ALL
YOU
CAN
EAT

Stories

Robin
Hemley

THE ATLANTIC MONTHLY PRESS
NEW YORK
•

Published simultaneously in Canada
Printed in the United States of America

Library of Congress Cataloging-in-Publication Data

Hemley, Robin, 1958–
All you can eat: stories / Robin Hemley.—1st ed.
ISBN 0-87113-261-3
I. Title.
PS3558.E47915A79   1988   88-14186
813'.54—dc19

The Atlantic Monthly Press
19 Union Square West
New York, NY 10003

FIRST PRINTING

For

Beverly

I wish to make grateful acknowledgment to the following organizations for their generous support: The Fine Arts Work Center in Provincetown, The MacDowell Colony, The Ragdale Foundation, The Illinois Arts Council, The Edward Albee Foundation, PEN American Center, and the Ohioana Library Association.

I am grateful to the following publications in which some of these stories first appeared: *ACM* (Another Chicago Magazine), *New Letters, Oink!, Shankpainter, Telescope, Wisconsin Review* and *20 Under 30: Best Short Stories by America's New Young Writers.*

Some of these stories appeared previously in *The Mouse Town* from Word Beat Press.

I would like to thank the following people who gave me their encouragement and support: Elaine Gottlieb, Lizzie Grossman, Anne Rumsey, Barry Silesky, and Sharon Solwitz.

Contents

All You
Can Eat

   Sarah, Jamie, and I are at
this pancake social given by a local church. Not that
we're churchgoers, it's just that we like pancakes. We
never use syrup though, only butter. Bad for our teeth,
you know. I remember when sweet meant good and
wholesome, but now you can't trust anything that
doesn't say "sugarless" or "all-natural" on the bottle.

   I didn't want to come here in the first place. In fact
when Sarah suggested it, I blew up. My weekends are
the only times I have to relax, and crowds of churchgoers aggravate me. I work hard at the office all week.
I'm up for promotion. Our marriage is going to hell.
Our son loves his toys more than us. And what does
Sarah want to do? She wants to go to a pancake social
just because Aunt Jemima is supposed to attend. The
Real Aunt Jemima.

   So what? I say. There's no such thing as the Real
Aunt Jemima anyway. There's probably a whole horde
of these Aunt Jemimas traveling around the country,
appearing at pancake socials. But my arguments have no
effect on Sarah. We never want to do the same things.
My idea of an enjoyable Sunday is staying home and
reading the newspaper, watching "Meet the Press" and
then "60 Minutes" later on. I'm the type of guy who

1

can't go a day without knowing what's going on in the world. If you wanted, you could quiz me and I'd know everything. Yesterday there was an earthquake in Peru, and it killed three hundred people.

Sarah, on the other hand, couldn't care less about news. All she's interested in is fixing up our house and taking Jamie to places like this. Last week it was the circus. The week before that she took the kid to one of those tacky little sidewalk sales called Art Daze. When we're alone together, we have nothing to say. I want to talk about Iran, and all she can think about is wood paneling in the den.

The meal is one of those all-you-can-eat deals. I've only had about four pancakes and I'm ready to go home, but I can't even suggest it because Aunt Jemima hasn't shown yet. All I can do is stare across the table at this fat man who's too busy pigging out to notice me. He's got his head bent so low to the table that his tie is soaking up the syrup on his plate. That's gluttony for you. As far as I'm concerned, gluttony is the worst sin by a long shot. And he's not the only one pigging out here. It seems like my family is the only one that knows how to eat decently.

The fat man sees me staring and lifts the corner of his mouth in a half smile. "You don't like pancakes?" he says, and adds, "This here's sure a bargain."

I don't have time to answer because the minister gets up on stage and announces that Aunt Jemima is here.

Out she comes, fat and dressed just like you see her on the syrup bottles: red polka-dotted kerchief, frowsy old dress, and a pair of tits that belong in a 4-H fair. The kids don't know who the hell she is, so they keep eating their pancakes like nothing's happening while the old

2

woman thanks everyone, especially the children, God's children, and tells us all how much she loves us.

Sarah leans over to my side and whispers, "I didn't realize she'd be such a racial stereotype."

"What do you expect of someone named Aunt Jemima?" I say.

The minister sits down at the piano, and Aunt Jemima turns around to tell him something, I suppose what key she's in. At that moment, all the parents grab the bottles of syrup on the table and show the kids just who Aunt Jemima is. When she turns around again, they go wild, now that they've seen her face on a mass-produced product. My Jamie starts to clap and yell along with all the others. Over the general roar in the church basement you hear a few parents telling their kids to eat their pancakes before they get cold.

"Before I start my song," says Aunt Jemima in a deep melodious voice, "I want to say a few words to y'all. Now I travel around the country singing to good folk like y'all, but I don't only sing, I have a message to bring. When you see me on a bottle of syrup, what do you really see? You don't just see old Aunt Jemima. You see all the things in life that's sweet and good, all them simple things in life, like maple syrup."

"Simple things in life," I tell Sarah. "Who's she fooling?"

"Relax, Jack," says Sarah. "If you'd stop acting like a skeptic for a minute, you might enjoy yourself. Just remember your blood pressure, okay?"

"I remember," I say. "I don't need you to remind me. But if I have a heart attack and drop dead, I want you to move my body. I don't want to be found dead among a bunch of churchgoers. Next she's going to start talking about family values."

But she doesn't. She goes right into her song, "He's Got the Whole World in His Hands." She's got a deep gospel voice and sways to the music while the minister accompanies her on that old piano with half the keys chipped away. While she sings, she makes motions with her hands. When she gets to the word *world*, she makes a circle. When she says *hands*, she cups her own together and looks piously up at the ceiling. After two verses, she stops and says, "Now I want all you children, God's children, to sing along with me and do all the things I do with my hands. Now when I say children, I don't just mean the young ones," and she gives us her famous syrupy smile. Everyone laughs, even me. I don't know, maybe there's not all that much difference between me and these churchgoers, and anyway, what's the use of arguing with such a sweet old woman? So I grab Sarah's hand, even though we just had an argument before breakfast, and she smiles at me like people do only in movies or rest homes, sort of vacant.

Sarah and I have had a lot of arguments recently. She's always reading these dumb women's magazines and trying out the things that they tell her to do. "101 Ways to Fix Chicken Pot Pie for the Man You Love," and stuff like that. Poor Sarah. She's been trying for the last fifteen years to make me happy, but the more she tries, the more bored I get with her. There are some people who aren't meant to be happy, and I'm one of them. I don't like happy people. Sarah is completely the opposite. Her favorite word is *tickle*. She likes to go to movies that tickle her, and if she ever reads a newspaper, it's only to scan the columnists who tickle her.

A couple of weekends ago, Sarah spent hours shellacking the covers of women's magazines onto the walls of our bathroom. Of course when I saw what she was doing, I was furious. "Sarah," I said. "This is the tackiest thing I've ever seen. I mean, you might as well turn the whole house into a 7-Eleven."

"I just thought it would brighten up the place," she said. "Don't you think it looks cheery?"

"It looks cheery as hell," I said. "I don't need cheeriness when I'm on the john."

Sarah sat down on the edge of the tub. Then she grabbed a pile of magazine covers, threw them over the drain, and turned on the water full blast. A model's face was on top, and the face just bounced up and down under the water pressure like it was doing some kind of strange facial swimming stroke.

For the first time in a while, I was scared for Sarah. I had an aunt who killed herself with sleeping pills, and this seemed to be just the kind of thing someone would do before they offed themselves. So I gave in. I let her shellac the bathroom so that now it looks like a newsstand. Then I took her out to dinner, and I didn't even mention the fact that the Soviet Union had rejected our latest arms proposal, though it was on my mind.

Now Sarah's acting like we've never argued in our lives. She's just giving me that silly smile of hers.

"I'm glad we came," I say to make her happy. "Pass the syrup."

"But you don't like syrup."

"That's true," I say. "I don't know what's come over me. It just looks so sweet, so wholesome."

"Daddy, can I have some syrup?" says Jamie.

"No. You remember your last checkup, don't you?"

"Oh, let him have some," says Sarah. "A little couldn't hurt," and she smiles at me. But she doesn't need to smile. Her hair smiles for her, flipping up on either side of her face, a phony style that went out fifteen years ago.

"Well, it *does* look good," I say. I pour some onto my pancakes and take a bite.

Yum.

Aunt Jemima's well into her song again, and everyone is singing along, following her motions with their hands. When she gets to the part about the "itty bitty baby in His hands," they all rock their arms back and forth. Some of the younger children don't know how to rock a baby and look more like they're sawing some object in half.

Babies. Sarah's wanted to have another child for a while, but I don't. She's so old-fashioned about that sort of thing. If I tried to tell her about exponential population growth and about starvation, she wouldn't understand me at all. She'd probably just smile and say, "But we're not some starving tribe in Africa, honey. We can afford another child." I've known Sarah long enough to know this is exactly what she'd say.

But it's all right. This anger towards Sarah will pass. Right now, I feel happy and know that the whole audience is thinking the same thought: everything is fine. We're all safe together in the hands of this fat old woman. She looks like she could shelter us from anything.

The shy-looking minister at the piano feels it too. He's pounding his fingers up and down on the keyboard, his skinny churchgoing rump half off the bench just like Jerry Lee Lewis. And the whole plaster ceiling is shaking, bits of it raining down on us like God's white teeth. Then the song ends, and everyone is tired and sweating. My brain is sweating from all this thinking. Maybe I should stop thinking and relax, like Sarah says.

I smell my armpits. That roll-on antiperspirant I use really *does* last a long time. As the commercial says, men sweat more than women, but you couldn't tell it by old

Aunt Jemima. She's got two wide circles around her armpits, and she says, "It's a mite hot in here."

Everyone agrees. All this combined body heat makes the place hotter than an oven. I look over at Jamie. In between songs, he's wolfing down pancakes like he's never tasted food before. And the syrup. His pancakes are swimming in it. Empty bottles line our long table like dominoes, and our waiter is working his butt off bringing stacks of steaming hot pancakes and bottles of maple syrup to everyone. I've never seen Jamie eat like this. Sarah and I have to feed him protein pills just to keep him from going anemic on us.

And that fat man. He's sure getting his money's worth. I've never seen anyone put away this much food.

I don't know what it is with him and me. We've been having this silent fight ever since we sat down, with him just smiling that weird half smile at me. I don't know why I feel so hostile toward this particular fat man. Maybe it's really guilt. Maybe I'm hostile because I have a lot of fat inside *me*, not the kind you can weigh. I'm really a skinny guy. Invisible fat.

"I sure wish Jamie would eat like this all the time," I tell Sarah.

"Me too," she says. "Maybe we should feed him pancakes morning, noon, and night." She sends me another vacant smile that doesn't mean anything. It's just polite. I look around the room and half the people in here have that same polite smile on their faces.

Anyway, what's she saying? Morning, noon, and night. I don't know about that.

I pour milk into my coffee with a moo-cow creamer, which is sort of disgusting if you think about it. I mean, the people who invented these things must have known that it looks like the cow is puking into your coffee.

I take a few bites of my pancakes, swishing them

around in the syrup with my fork. Yum, yum. They're such simple things really, brown on the outside, fluffy white inside. But they're so good. I never realized before that covering them with syrup makes all the difference in the world.

Aunt Jemima is singing another song now, called "Pancake Lady." None of us know the words, so we just let her sing while we laugh along in between bites.

> Pancake Lady makes pancakes for me
> Pancake Lady makes pancakes for free
> Eat 'em up, eat 'em up, one, two, three
> Pancake Lady's got a hold on me

Suddenly Jamie gags and yells with his mouth full, "Look, there's a fly in my pancake. Yuck, there's a fly in my pancake."

Sure enough, Jamie's fork has uncovered a little fly, snugly wedged in a piece of white fluff, its itty feet and its bitty head sticking out.

"Jamie," says Sarah. "Don't make such a fuss over a little fly. You're going to spoil everyone's breakfast."

"Your mother's right," I say. "Have some more syrup and eat your pancakes."

"But I'm not hungry anymore. It's gross. A gross, dead fly in my pancake."

As soon as Jamie says gross, the fat man looks over at him with a pained expression. I put my arm around Jamie's shoulder and hug him to me so that his mouth is squeezed into my armpit. I smile at the fat man and whisper to Jamie, "You're embarrassing me, you little twit. Finish your pancakes or you won't eat for a month."

Jamie's mouth is so firmly planted in my armpit he can barely move his lips. "Daddy, you're hurting me," says a voice like the dummy of an amateur ventriloquist.

8

All You Can Eat

The fat man leans across the table and pokes his fork at my son. "Nice little boy you got there," he says. And then he does something disgusting. He sticks out his fat cow tongue, covered with big chunks of chewed-up pancakes. If he wasn't an adult, I'd think he had shown me his slimy food on purpose.

"Oh yes," I say, a little flabbergasted. "He is kind of nice. Jamie, thank the nice fat man."

Oh shit, I didn't mean to say that. I look at the fat man, but he's just smiling at me, taking big bites from his stack of pancakes.

"Daddy," says Jamie, his voice like the sound of a TV in another room. "Please let me go. I'll eat anything."

I free Jamie and tell him, "Now be a good boy and eat your pancakes and syrup."

Jamie looks all right, just a little red in the face. He picks up his fork, pours syrup on his pancakes, and then makes a big ceremony of cutting away the piece with the fly. He slides it with his fork to the side of his plate.

"His mother spoils him," I tell the fat man, and Sarah gives me a "wait until we get home" look.

I glance at Sarah and wonder why she still wears her hair in that phony flip that went out of style fifteen years ago. I just wish we had something like syrup to pour on our marriage.

Yesterday we were talking for the millionth time about having a kid, and I said, "Look, I bet you don't even know who the prime minister of Japan is."

"Maybe I don't," she said. "But that's because I don't bury myself in things that don't matter."

"The world doesn't matter?" I said.

When Sarah argues, she gets irrational. All she did to answer me was to recite this kids' rhyme, "Here's the church, here's the steeple. Open the doors and see all the people." She also made the corresponding motions

9

with her hands, first interlocking her fists, then pointing her index fingers into a spire, and then opening up her hands and wiggling her fingers at me. After that she stuck out her tongue and locked herself in the bathroom. A woman like that certainly can't handle another child. Still, there was something sort of endearing about her at that moment.

Aunt Jemima finishes the song and we all clap for her. I wonder where she's been for the last fifteen years. Things sure do seem a lot simpler when she's around.

I look over at the fat man for a second. This time he looks me directly in the eye, and with a wink, opens his mouth as wide as it will go, showing me a mouthful of stuff that looks like foam rubber.

"Listen, mattress-face," I say. "I've had just about enough of you," and I get ready to send him a punch, though I'm sure he's got enough flesh in that shock-absorbing face to suck up half my arm. I'm halfway off the bench and across the table when Aunt Jemima starts into her next song, "Camptown Races." As soon as I hear that soothing voice, I just can't get up enough energy to be angry anymore. I float back nice and easy to my bench, like a paper cut-out doll.

I lean over to Sarah and whisper, "Speaking of racial stereotypes, what do you think of this one?"

"It's lovely," she says, smiling at me and blinking like she's in some 1960's beach party movie.

Aunt Jemima tells everyone to sing with her, and so we sing.

The kids love this song. Most of them don't know the words, but they sing along anyway. They especially love the line, Doo dah, doo dah, and won't sing anything but these words. The song soon turns into a shouting match among the children, most of them substituting Doo dah, and then Doo doo, for all the words in between. I sort of resent this alteration of the original, but no one else seems to mind. Aunt Jemima looks like she's having a blast, dancing around the stage like a voodoo queen, her enormous hands waving in front of her.

The fat man is yelling Doo doo in my face.

Plaster chips fall from the ceiling as the song ends, and with hardly a break, Aunt Jemima leads us in "The Hokey Pokey." The minister's hands flop up and down on the keyboard like a marionette's. Everyone rises from the benches and crowds in between the tables to do the Hokey Pokey dance. There's not enough room for a circle, so we make two lines facing each other. Like two Zulu armies dancing before a battle, we shake our feet, then our hands, and then we turn ourselves around.

Aunt Jemima's voice rises above us, singing, "That's what it's all about."

I am suddenly disturbed by the fact that I am shaking my hands and feet at the command of an old woman. If someone from the office were to come in now I would certainly be passed over for promotion. They'd make life unbearable. "Glad you're working for us," they'd say. "We need a man around the firm who knows his Hokey Pokey."

But I can't stop doing the dance. This is ten times better than watching "Meet the Press." It's hard to worry about work, divorce, or even the world when you're doing the Hokey Pokey.

When the song finally ends, everyone in the church basement groans. We want more, but Aunt Jemima says she's tired. In fact she looks completely drained. Her kerchief has fallen off, and she doesn't even have enough strength to pick it up. But we want an encore.

11

The crowd's past control, with everyone shouting and hooting for more.

"I'm about ready for some more pancakes and syrup," I tell Sarah over the noise.

"Daddy?" says Jamie. "I'm tired. Can we go home?"

"We'll go home when I say so," I tell him. "We can't leave in the middle of Miss Jemima's last song. She'd be offended."

"You're good people," Aunt Jemima tells us. "Real fine people. Now before I sing my last song, I want to ask you, what's the best food in the whole wide world?"

"Pancakes!" we yell.

"And what tastes better on pancakes than anything else?"

"Syrup!"

Why, there's nothing we wouldn't eat for this fine woman.

With tears in her eyes, she leads us once again in "He's Got the Whole World in His Hands." We're still standing from the Hokey Pokey, and so we sway along.

When she says world, we all make a globe. When she says hands, we cup our hands like we're holding robins' eggs.

Then she sings, "He's got you and me brother in His hands," and clutches her chest. We all clutch our chests. She collapses on the floor, and everyone except for the minister at the piano collapses with her.

Lying on the floor like that, we sing until all the verses are done.

After the song ends, the basement is quiet except for our breathing. Slowly, we rise to our feet, all except Aunt Jemima, who remains on the floor, her arms folded on her chest, her eyes closed. She's quite a gal, joking around like that.

The minister gets up from his piano bench, steps

12

over Aunt Jemima, and yells, "Three cheers for Aunt Jemima."

We all cheer, but she's so modest, she doesn't even respond. She just stays on the floor, that syrupy smile fixed on the ceiling.

I sit down with the rest of the crowd.

Then the waiters spring out of the kitchen, carrying trays of steaming hot pancakes and new bottles of syrup, and we begin to eat again. I have a voracious appetite. So does Jamie. He's shoveling pancakes into his mouth. The piece with the fly is gone. He must have eaten it. In fact, everyone is eating with so much gusto that no one has time to talk. All you can hear is the *squish squish* of people chewing pancakes, like the sound of an army walking in wet shoes.

People are smiling and laughing. I smile at Sarah. That hair style of hers is the most attractive thing in the world right now, except of course, for pancakes with lots of syrup.

I lean her way and say, "I've been thinking, Sarah. I've changed my mind. Let's have a baby."

"Let's have lots and lots of babies," she says.

"Gobs and gobs of babies."

"Daddy?" says Jamie with a cute expression of concern on his face. "If you have lots and lots of babies, will you still love me?"

"Why certainly, young man. That's what it's all about."

"Ooh Daddy," he says. "I love you as much as pancakes."

"With lots of syrup," I reply. "That reminds me. I could use some more."

I ask the nice man across the table to pass the syrup, and he kindly obliges. Then I see that a couple of paramedics have come to take Aunt Jemima away. No one else seems to notice. Maybe I'll find out what happened to her on the news, but then again, maybe I won't. I'm sure she'll be all right. I don't know, it's just a feeling I have, that all of us are safe together.

The Mouse Town

Mitch and I were friends by pure chance, and the wonderful world of torture might never have opened up to us if not for the deaths of our fathers. After all, we were the only kids at Pitman Elementary School with dead dads, though they had died in different ways.

Mitch's dad was a helicopter pilot in Vietnam, and had flown too close to hill #464 rather than 465. While 465 was a friendly hill, 464 was not. It was occupied by the Vietcong, who blew him away as he headed his chopper toward the ground.

My dad died of a heart attack. He was forty-five, a professor at Ohio University, a nervous, chain-smoking, overweight man. Late one night, while grading papers, he told my mother he didn't feel well. Before I knew it, he was in the hospital. My mother woke me up and sent me to the Handys'. She must have known that Dad was going to die or she wouldn't have sent me to the house of a dead man. She and Mrs. Handy knew each other, but you couldn't call them close friends. My mother didn't have close friends, only my father and me.

Mrs. Handy and my mother knew each other because Mitch and I were in the same class, and because my mother had her hair done at Mrs. Handy's home beauty salon. I liked staying with the Handys, even though I couldn't stand the beauty salon smell. Mrs. Handy allowed me to skip school, watch "Mission Impossible," and eat Jiffy Pop popcorn.

At the end of the week my father died, but I didn't cry when Mrs. Handy told me. I just went outside and played a giant game of World War on the front lawn with my G.I. Joes. When Mitch got home from school that day, I tried to tell him of my father's death, but couldn't get it out. I started to laugh, even though I didn't know what was so hilarious. And then Mitch laughed, too. Mrs. Handy didn't know what to make of us.

When I returned to school, Mrs. Wallace, my third grade teacher, told the class they had to be nice to me. Mitch didn't have to be nice to me because I had been staying at his house, and he already knew the whole situation. Instead, he strutted around the halls, pointing me out to other kids and telling them that his father had died, too.

Of all my classmates, a girl named Laura was the nicest. I kept twenty-six mice in an aquarium at school, and Laura, without anyone's urging, gave me a mouse town made entirely out of cardboard and construction paper. It had a cardboard foundation, a street down the middle, and four houses and stores on either side. Each house or store had at least two stories and four rooms. There was a mouse bank, a mouse bar, a mouse market, and a mouse funeral home.

I wanted to try it out immediately. Mitch did, too, and was jealous of my good fortune. So I invited him to sleep over at my house. We grabbed a mouse from the aquarium, a black one named George, and took the bus home.

After dinner we set the mouse town on the living

16

room floor and put George inside. My mother watched us silently from the couch. In the two weeks since my father's death, she hadn't gone out in public or received any guests. Now, as we played, she smiled and said not to mind her. But I didn't want her hanging around. We couldn't explore all the mouse town's possibilities with her in the room.

I suggested to Mitch that we play somewhere else, and so he grabbed George by the tail and I carried the mouse town up to my bedroom.

When I shut the bedroom door I said, "Okay, now we can play. Let's put George in the funeral home so he can see his dad."

I seized George and dragged him down the street in jerky motions. George didn't know what was going on. He stuck out his front legs and clawed the cardboard while I acted his part. "DOO! Do-do doo do do," I sang to the tune of "Stop, in the Name of Love."

"Let's see what they got at the funeral home today," I said.

Mitch grabbed one of my G.I. Joes off the floor, where it lay with its legs curled in a semi-lotus position and its arms sticking straight up over its head. Mitch straightened out its arms and legs and planted G.I. Joe in front of the funeral home.

"Hi, George Mouse," he said. "What do you want?"

I pinned George's tail to the cardboard with my index finger while he tried to run in the opposite direction.

"Not much," I said. "What you got inside?"

"Dead people," said Mitch. "You want to see them?"

"Sure," I said, and Mitch took Joe away from the door. I shoved George inside and yelled in a mousey, high-pitched voice. "Oh, no, it's my dad."

George didn't like where I had placed him. He stuck his head outside the door, looked up and down the street, his whiskers twitching in panic, and tore away from the funeral home. A moment later he disappeared into the saloon.

My mother burst into the room, glancing up and down with the same panicked expression as George, and said, "What's wrong? I heard you yell."

"Nothing's wrong," I said. "We were just playing."

"Are you sure you're all right?" she said. "Would you like some cookies and milk?"

"Great," said Mitch, looking up at her for the first time.

"Just give me cookies," I said.

"But you need something to wash them down with."

"Okay, a Coke."

"Mrs. Irving," said Mitch. "Get me a Coke, too. A Coke and a glass of milk."

When she shut the door, Mitch said, "Let's make believe George is a paratrooper and has to get the body of his dad back from the Vietcong."

"Great," I said. I lifted one side of the mouse town and shook George out of the saloon, sliding him into the mouse market. I grabbed him before he could run away.

"Let's use your pillowcase for a parachute," said Mitch. Without waiting for an answer, he went to my bed and shook the pillowcase from my pillow. Then he opened it up and told me to put George inside. When this was done, he closed the pillowcase and started swinging it around his head.

"Mayday, Mayday," he said. "Jet out of control. Request permission to jump."

Mitch's eyes were blazing as he whipped the air with his arm. I thought George was done for. I was sure

18

Mitch was going to slam him into the wall. But then his arm started slowing down, and after a few sweeps, he set the pillowcase in the middle of the mouse town.

I shook George out of the pillowcase to see if he was dead. As soon as he was out, he wobbled back on his hind legs, regained his balance, and made a dash for it. But I swiped him up with my hand and said, "That's fun. Let me try."

I dumped George back in the pillowcase, stood up, and swung him around my head. When he had reached maximum velocity, my mother opened the door, saw what I was doing, and almost dropped her tray of milk, cookies, and Coke.

I stopped swinging George and set the pillowcase on the floor. My mother stood bewildered by the door, watching the little lump in the pillowcase make its way to the opening. As soon as George was free, he ran under my bed.

My mother set down her tray and ran over to me. She took me by the shoulders and shook me with a violence I had never seen in her before. "You little brat," she screamed.

I started to cry, and kept repeating, "We were just having fun. Just fun."

*A*fter the incident with George, Mitch and I no longer tortured my mice in front of my mother. Still, we had fun when she wasn't around. As time went by, my mice became testier, biting us, attacking each other, and looking over their shoulders to see if we were around.

During these months, our mothers were becoming

closer, even though they seemed to have little in common outside of their widowhood.

One night toward the beginning of Christmas vacation, I overheard my mother arguing with Mrs. Handy over the phone. I was already in bed when I heard my mother's voice raised. I quietly got up, put on my bathrobe, and tiptoed to the kitchen. The last time I had been awakened in such a way was the night my father was sent to the hospital.

My mother stood in the bright kitchen light, one hand clutching the receiver, the other clenched in a fist as though she wanted to strike the phone. The strangest thing was the party dress she wore, a dress I hadn't seen on her since my father was alive. She also wore a necklace and high heels.

She seemed embarrassed and awkward in her good clothes, looking around the room nervously as though she knew I was there. I had to keep ducking around the corner to keep her from seeing me.

"I can't, Yvonne," she said into the phone. "I've changed my mind."

Even across the room I could hear Mrs. Handy's reply. "I'm just trying to help," she said in a screechy voice.

"I'm sorry, Yvonne," my mother said softly. "I know you're trying to help, but it just wouldn't work out."

Mrs. Handy's reply was soft and garbled.

"I *am* thinking of myself," said my mother, her voice rising again. "Besides, I couldn't find a sitter for Danny."

"But they're waiting for us," said Mrs. Handy. "Right now. It's just not polite."

"I told you I've changed my mind."

"But you can't," said Mrs. Handy, speaking loud

20

enough to match my mother. "Don't be so selfish. What am I supposed to do with two of them?"

I couldn't figure out why my mother was upset. I didn't know where Mrs. Handy wanted to take her, or who was waiting for them. I imagined Mrs. Handy forcing my mother to go somewhere awful like the dentist. I didn't want to see my mother cry, so I left the kitchen and tiptoed back to my bedroom. Before I fell asleep I heard my mother's voice grow shriller, and I heard her yell, "Not now, not yet. Can't you understand?" I buried myself under my covers and imagined all my mother's teeth falling out.

Mitch and I weren't allowed to play together after that. Over Christmas vacation I brought all my mice home with me. My favorite activity during this time was building fires in the fireplace. Usually I wasn't allowed to play with matches, but for some reason my mother was becoming less strict.

After the fire was going, I would set several plastic green soldiers at various points on the logs, and then try to save each man before the fire reached him. Sometimes I was unsuccessful, and would watch helplessly as their faces sizzled and turned black. Even so, I was fascinated by their deaths. They danced as they died, a slow graceful cross between a ballet and the twist. Their machine guns would droop and drip onto their legs. Then their arms would distend and attach to the logs, and finally the soldiers would take a long deep bow.

But it wasn't the same without Mitch. One night I decided to call him and invite myself to sleep over that weekend.

"Mitch," I said when Mrs. Handy had given him the phone. "I got a great idea for an experiment with the mice."

"What is it?" He sounded happy, but cautious. I knew that Mrs. Handy was standing right beside him.

"I can't tell you now. Can I come over on Saturday and sleep over?"

"Sure," he said. "I'll ask Mom." A moment later, he returned to the phone. "Mom says it's all right if it's all right with your mom."

I went into my mother's bedroom where she was lying on her bed propped against two pillows. "Mom?" I said. "Can I spend Saturday night with the Handys? Mitch's mom says it's all right if it's all right with you."

"Doesn't she want to speak to me?" she said.

"I don't know. I'll go ask."

"No, never mind," she said. "Tell him it's fine."

Saturday my mother drove me to the Handys' place, a whitewashed house with front and back porches. I stepped out of the car holding my mouse town. Inside the mouse town was a cage with four mice, including the veteran, George.

Before my mother could drive away, Mrs. Handy opened the porch door and waved. She was dressed in a bathrobe, and the sudden gush of winter air made her do a small jig.

"Lana," she yelled cheerily. "Come in. There's someone I want you to meet. Come on before I catch my death."

I was hoping my mother wouldn't go inside. If she got going on the subject of my dad, I knew she'd embarrass me in front of Mitch, either by crying or calling me over to her side and hugging me.

My mother saw what I was thinking, and said, "I've got to go home, Yvonne."

"Come on," said Mrs. Handy. "Just for a cup of coffee. I want to know all you been up to. I ain't seen you in an age."

After a while, my mother gave in. I went in the house before her to give Mitch the impression we had nothing to do with each other.

The odor of Mrs. Handy's salon hit me immediately. The salon was adjacent to the living room, and you could see two rows of dryers and wash basins from the doorway. The smell was overwhelming, something like sweet and sour sauce. It hung around the top of your mouth until you were forced to swallow.

The living room was a mess, beauty magazines scattered around, a TV sitting on concrete blocks, and old furniture with the varnish chipped off. Besides Mitch and his mother, there was a man sitting on the couch, watching TV. He look like he belonged there, though I had never met him before.

"Mitch has just been dying to see you," Mrs. Handy said to me in her Appalachian twang.

My mother entered the room, and Mrs. Handy took her by the hand and led her to the couch, where she said, "This here is who I want you to meet. Jack, this is my dear friend, Lana."

Mitch was lying on the floor, watching TV. "What you got?" he said.

"Not much," I answered. "Just the mice."

"Jack is my boyfriend," said Mrs. Handy with the air of someone showing off a new car.

My mother responded to Mrs. Handy's remark with a bewildered smile. The man on the couch was young and handsome, except for two deformities. He had a neck like an ostrich, long and thin with stubble sticking out. He also had a lower lip which protruded from the rest of his mouth like a permanent pout. Actually, the second time you looked at the guy, you thought he wasn't handsome in a normal sort of way, but handsome in an ugly sort of way, like G.I. Joe.

"He looks like quite a catch," said my mother, as if she were talking about a fish.

"Don't say that," said Mrs. Handy, shoo-shooing her hands in front of her face. "I ain't caught him yet."

"Mitch," said the man on the couch. "Tell your friend to move his head. I can't see." He had an Appalachian twang, too, and pronounced "can't" as "kate."

"Better move your head," said Mitch without looking at me. A Japanese sub had just landed on Gilligan's Island. It looked like trouble.

"Yvonne needs a man around here," said the man on the couch, and then gave Mrs. Handy a bitter look, like he had just swallowed some of that sweet and sour air.

"That Jap thinks it's World War Two," said Mitch. "Think they'll blow him up and steal his sub?"

"Danny needs someone, too," said my mother, but she looked as though she wasn't paying attention to what she was saying. Her voice was soft, and she wasn't looking at any of us. She stared at the ceiling and then down at her lap.

"They won't steal his sub," I said. "If they did, they'd get off the island. Let's watch 'My Mother the Car.' "

"Don't you worry, dear," said Mrs. Handy. "Things'll get better in a year. They did for me," and she smiled at her man, who wasn't paying attention. Then she added, "You'll find someone for sure in a year."

"Mitch," said the man on the couch. "Tell your friend if he wants to change the channel, he kate."

Mrs. Handy looked at me and shriveled up her

nose. "Danny's taking it well. In my opinion, he's been a little man all through it."

"Let's play with the mouse town," I suggested to Mitch. "You got any matches?"

"What for?" he said.

"I'll tell you in a minute."

Mitch stood up and went to the couch. "You got any matches, Jack?"

"I'll go get some coffee," said Mrs. Handy, smiling proudly at the pretty picture of Jack and Mitch. "See how well they get along?" she said to my mother, and she disappeared into the kitchen.

The man handed Mitch a pack of matches, craning his head around so that he could watch the show uninterrupted.

I pretended I didn't see what Mitch was doing. My mother couldn't very well scold somebody else's son for having fun.

As soon as Mitch returned I said, "Let's go to the back porch," and I grabbed the mouse town with the mice inside the cage.

"Yvonne," my mother yelled toward the kitchen. "Is Mitch allowed to play with matches?"

"Don't worry about *my* son," said Mrs. Handy. "He'll be fine." And then she yelled to Mitch, "Honey, don't start any fires in here."

"Yes, Mom," he answered, and we ran through the beauty room to the back porch.

"Come here," I said, stepping outside into the cold, fresh-smelling air.

"What we gonna do?" he said.

"We're going to burn the mouse town," I said.

"With the mice in it?" His eyes lit up.

"Yeah."

"Great," he said, and we both quickly cleared snow from a patch of ground at the bottom of the steps. Then we set the mouse town on top of it.

We took the mice out of the cage one by one, and placed them at various points in the town. We put one in the second story of the mouse market, another in the mouse bank, another in one of the mouse houses, and George in the farthest room of the mouse funeral home. The cold air made the mice dumber than usual, and they stayed where we put them, all except for George, who kept trying to find a way out. Of all my mice, George had gone through the most tortures. We had tied a parachute to him and dropped him from a small tree. We had given him swimming lessons. And once we had put him in the seat of a hollowed-out plastic car, and sent him careening down the steepest hill in town, clutching the dashboard and silently screaming all the way.

We had made George volunteer for all these missions because he was our favorite mouse.

I struck a match and lit one of the bottom corners of the mouse funeral home. The cardboard slowly took fire, turning blue and then peeling upward like a theater curtain.

Mitch took a match and lit the mouse market. When the fire got close to the mouse funeral home, I said, "Oh, oh, someone's started a fire. We've got to do something."

"Do something quick," yelled Mitch with glee, at the same time lighting the roof of one of the mouse houses.

I ripped off the roof of the funeral home and saw George sitting in a corner, the fire working its way toward him. I grabbed him by the tail and plucked him out. Then I replaced the roof.

26

"Saved," I yelled.

"Good work," said Mitch. "You'll get a medal for this."

I shook Mitch's hand and shoved George back into the funeral home. He didn't want to go and ran back out.

"No," I said, picking up George by his tail. "You've got to find your wife. She's in there somewhere."

I placed George in the mouse saloon, a safe place for the time being. "Have a drink," I suggested. "We'll find her for you."

"What maniac has set our town on fire?" Mitch said.

"We'll worry about that later," I said. "Right now, we've got to save everybody."

The mouse market was blazing, and so Mitch tore a hole in the wall and stuck his hand inside. A moment later he withdrew it. "Ow, it bit me. Let it die."

I ran over to Mitch's side of the town and ripped off the roof of the mouse market. Then I stuck my hand inside and grabbed the mouse.

"Safe," I yelled.

"Let me save one," Mitch said, still rubbing his finger.

I placed the other mouse in the saloon with George, its husband.

"Darling," I said. "I thought you were dead."

"Darling," Mitch replied, getting back into the spirit of things. "Don't worry. We're safe in here," Then he lit the saloon in three separate places.

"Here comes the fire engine," I said, and dumped a handful of snow on the burning mouse market. The fire subsided a bit, and so I took a mouse out of the mouse bank and stuck it inside the market.

Then I lit it again.

We continued to burn the mouse town down. Each

time a fire got close to a mouse, we saved it and put it in another burning building. The mice were brave and dignified for the most part.

Finally there were no more fires to start. Every building was burning. The walls of the mouse town were crumbling and the roofs were starting to cave in. The wind caught grey ashes and swept them away. I decided it was time to save the mice once and for all.

"We better get them out before they die," I suggested.

"Yeah, we better," said Mitch sullenly.

"You know where they all are?" I said.

"I think so."

We knew where two of them were for sure. We took one of them from the mouse bank and another from the mouse saloon. As soon as we had put them back in their cage, a third mouse appeared in the doorway of the mouse market. It hesitated for a second, and then ran down the street and jumped into the snowbank at the edge of the town. Mitch grabbed the mouse and placed it in the cage with its buddies.

"That's three," I said. "Where's George?"

"I don't know," he said.

We were both frightened, and started ripping the burning roofs off the buildings. We still couldn't find George, even after we had torn away every roof. So we threw snow on the mouse town, flinging handfuls at the cardboard structures.

"Hurry up," I yelled frantically. "We've got to save George."

But the fire was too strong. The snow didn't do much good. In a last ditch effort, I stuck my hand in the lower story of the blazing mouse saloon, groping around as the fire closed in on my fingers. I felt George's tail, and I lunged for him, closing my fist around his body.

Withdrawing my hand before I got burned, I yelled, "Got him!"

"Is he all right?" Mitch said, concerned.

I opened up my hand and looked at him. "Are you all right, George?" I said.

He peed in my hand.

After I had returned George to his cage, Mitch and I covered the mouse town with snow. Mitch turned to me and said, "Did you get burned?"

"Nope," I said proudly.

"Say yes," Mitch insisted, "and you'll get a Purple Heart."

"Okay," I said, smiling.

"Danny?" Mitch said. "We have fun together, don't we?"

"Sure," I said.

"I've got a secret to tell you," he said.

"What is it?"

"My mom don't like your mom."

"I know," I said. I also knew that my mother didn't like Mrs. Handy, and I couldn't understand why they pretended they were friends.

"I got another secret to tell you," Mitch said.

"What is it?"

"That guy in there ain't my mom's sweetheart. He's my Uncle Bill. My mom wants to fool your mom, but she made me promise I wouldn't tell."

We walked into the house, arms around each other's shoulders. When we entered the living room, we were smiling big mischievous grins.

"You have fun?" said Mrs. Handy.

"Plenty," I answered.

The man on the couch was watching "Bewitched."
My mother stood by the doorway, her hand on the
knob. When I saw that she was about to leave, I was
suddenly afraid. I didn't want her to leave me alone.

She looked at me and smiled. I ran to her and burst
into tears. "Mom," I yelled. "I'm burned. My hand got
burned," and I clenched one of my hands with the
other.

Mrs. Handy was unsympathetic. "That's what you
get for playing with matches," she said.

But my mother didn't even tell Mrs. Handy to shut
up. She didn't pay any attention to her at all. I was the
only person she saw in that room. She bent down,
gently lifted my hand from the imaginary wound, and
smiled. Then she pointed to a spot on my palm and
said, "Is this where it hurts?"

Clues

A little lost as he walked to work early one morning, Gerald Kemp wandered into a neighborhood he had never seen. Drab bungalows with the paint peeling off their sides surrounded him, and no one was in the street. But as he was passing one of the houses a door opened and a young boy came out on the stoop, cradling a bowling ball in his arms. The boy looked to his right and then to his left, and set the ball on the top step. The ball started to roll a little, but he stopped it with his foot. Then he went back inside the house and slowly closed the door.

When Gerald saw this, he slackened his pace. This was exactly the kind of thing that people who drove to work never saw. It was a little like a dream, and as he continued on his way, he felt a bit lightheaded and happy. That's the way unusual things affected him.

After a few minutes he stopped trying to figure out what it meant, and by the afternoon he'd completely forgotten about the boy and the bowling ball.

The next morning as he was walking he found a dime on the sidewalk. The dime was dated with the year of his birth and was slightly discolored and had a couple of nicks as though someone had chewed on it. This was the type of thing that other people missed in the city because of the way they hurried around. He closed his palm around the coin and thought of a wish, and for a moment he had complete faith in the dime he'd found.

"I want something important to happen to me today," he thought and put the dime in his pocket.

The next thing he noticed was a black squirrel in a tree. He hadn't seen a black squirrel since he was a boy in Iowa. When he saw it, he stopped and said, "Fantastic," assuming that this was the answer to his wish. He clucked his tongue and tried to make the squirrel come down, but it just started chewing on something and looked at him suspiciously.

After a few moments he gave up. He walked about a block, and as he was passing by a townhouse, the front door opened. A woman who looked like she was in her forties stood there in a nightgown. As he passed her he smiled, but she just followed him glumly with her eyes. He had almost gone by the house when she stepped back inside the door, bent down, and set something on the stoop. A bowling ball. He stopped and looked at the woman, who looked back with the same glum expression. Then she turned around and walked inside her house. A moment later the door closed.

Gerald walked back to the iron gate that surrounded her place. He looked through the fence at the ball, which had three holes. Definitely a bowling ball. He started to undo the gate, but saw the curtains move, and so he let the latch drop.

He walked a little farther along. Another door opened. An elderly man stumbled out onto his steps as though he had been pushed. He looked fairly distinguished with a white mustache and silvery hair. He was gaunt and had a tired expression.

He also had a bowling ball in his hands.

Gerald hurried closer so he could catch the man before he disappeared inside his house.

"Excuse me."

The man stood up straight and looked at Gerald.

Clues

"Why are you carrying that bowling ball?" Gerald said.

The old man looked at the bowling ball in his hands, as though he didn't know why he had it either. Then he put the ball down on the stoop, stood back, and gave it a kick. The ball barely moved, and the man looked over at Gerald in pain.

Gerald moved a little closer to see if the man was hurt, but as soon as he took a step the old man limped inside and slammed the door.

Gerald walked up to the door and heard a deadbolt snap. He knocked but there was no answer. He pounded on the door, but still no one opened up. He turned around and looked down at the bowling ball. The ball was a little chipped, old and unpolished, like it wasn't someone's personal ball, but a common one that had been used by countless others.

He stood there for a minute looking at the ball. Then he bent down and put his fingers inside the three holes. The holes fit his fingers perfectly. He picked the ball up and swung it back and forth a couple of times. It was the right weight for him too. He looked across the street and imagined a set of pins there. He felt like throwing the ball. There was power there, and he thought he could knock down anything that stood in his way. He tried to imagine people he knew falling in front of him: his co-workers, his boss, a woman to whom he had once been engaged, his younger brother, and his parents.

During the years he had spent in Iowa before coming to the city, his family had gone bowling every Friday night at a place called the Colonial Lanes, where neon people in eighteenth-century dress hung on the walls. Gerald had always hated bowling, but only now realized that he hated it. At the time he had thought he

33

liked bowling because his mother and father and younger brother all liked to bowl. He remembered concentrating on the reflections of the pins. He remembered aiming his ball slightly off center, taking three steps and swinging. Most of all he remembered the sensation as he let the ball drop on the waxed wood of the lane, a sticky feeling in his hands, and the knowledge that he couldn't take the ball back now that he'd thrown it. The ball almost always veered off right or left and landed in the gutter or knocked down only a couple of pins. No matter how much he danced or swung his hands over to one side or turned his back, the ball was gone and had made up its own mind how many pins it was going to hit.

He hated bowling because it seemed controlled by fate. His parents were the ones who believed in fate. Gerald's father owned a lumberyard and had named his first son after him without any junior to clarify the family's lineage. His father was Gerald Kemp and he was Gerald Kemp too. When Gerald Kemp died, Gerald Kemp would take over the lumberyard, and his grandchildren, both boys and girls, would also be named Gerald Kemp, and they would crawl all over the spruce and mahogany like benign termites.

The younger Gerald Kemp had turned away from all that. For the last three years, he thought he had finally escaped the ball his father had thrown. But recently he had started to question the choice he had made. His younger brother, Gilbert, ran the lumber company now. Gilbert's wife was pregnant and was due any day, and Gerald was sure that they'd have a boy they'd call Gilbert without any junior behind it. This somehow made him feel as though he'd been cheated. His life in the city wasn't any more unpredictable than it had been in the country. He'd come here to find new

Clues

things, but he hadn't really found that much. Just old dimes and black squirrels from his childhood.

Now he put the ball down and tried the door again, but there was still no answer.

So he walked a little farther down the block. As he was walking along, he saw a twenty-dollar bill. It was hanging off the edge of the sidewalk, finely balanced, and it looked wrinkled but untorn. For some reason the bill didn't interest him. In fact the sight of it made him hostile, and he kicked it down in the gutter.

He walked on a few feet and then decided he wasn't proving anything, so he turned around and retrieved the twenty-dollars. The bill was a little muddy now, and as he started walking again he tried to clean off the dirt with an old piece of tissue he had stuck in his back pocket. He wasn't really looking where he was going as he did this. He wiped off a thin black film the bill had picked up in the street. He took out his wallet and stuck the bill inside. As he was putting his wallet back in his pocket, he turned a corner and finally looked up to see where he was.

In front of him was a house with a bowling ball on the doorstep. As he walked past the next house, he glanced over at the stoop, but was relieved to see no bowling ball there.

But then the door opened, and an arm quickly sneaked a bowling ball onto the porch and closed the door again.

Gerald walked faster. As he came to each house or apartment building on the block, he saw that every one had a bowling ball sitting in front of it. But there weren't any people around, and there wasn't a sound on the block either. Usually you could hear the El screeching around a corner in the distance. Or the traffic on the main streets. Or the wind gusting along like a reckless

driver. But now there wasn't a sound from any direction, except for a slow rumble in the distance that he
couldn't quite make out.

He was about to turn around and bypass this entire
neighborhood, but then the rumble got louder. He just
stood there in the middle of the street, fascinated and
unable to move. Finally a truck turned the corner towards him. It looked like a garbage truck, and a man
was hanging from its back. The truck stopped at the
farthest house on the block and the man jumped off.

He looked about twenty. He had broad shoulders
and was wearing a red checked shirt that hung out of his
jeans. He walked to the closest house, right past the
garbage cans and up to the front stoop. He bent down,
picked up the bowling ball, and stood up again, swinging it loosely against his hip. In a moment he reached
the truck and threw the ball in the back. Then he went
to the next house, the truck following slowly behind
him.

Gerald went up to him and said in a friendly tone,
"Could you tell me what you're doing with all those
balls?"

The man ignored Gerald. He had another ball in his
hand and started walking back to the truck, but
changed course, and picked up another ball from the
next house. Now he was carrying two.

Gerald kept pace behind the man and repeated his
question, but again the man didn't answer. "Are you
recycling these balls or something?" he said. "I'm just
curious, that's all."

The man turned around and gave Gerald an ugly
look.

"I think I have a right to know," said Gerald, realiz-
ing at the same time that he didn't have a right to know.

Clues

The man threw one ball and then the other into the back of the truck.

"In any case," Gerald continued. "I'd like to know what you're doing and how much it costs to have it done. I might be interested. Not that I bowl that often. I'm really no good. But at least I'm active. I play racquetball on a semiregular basis, so maybe you could recommend some comparable service."

"This ain't no service," said the man without looking at him, and then he added, "Aren't you late for work or something?"

There was nothing more Gerald could do, so he turned from the man and walked away.

At the first intersection he came to, he waited for a cab. He was going to be late for work if he didn't get one. It was rush hour, and all the cabs that went by had passengers inside. Finally, after ten minutes, he caught sight of a cab with its light on and flagged it down.

The cabbie asked Gerald where he wanted to go, and he thought a moment. He felt he had a choice again for the first time since he'd come to the city. Screw work, he thought. Work was unimportant. It didn't matter whether he was late. It didn't matter whether he even showed up.

Instead of giving the cabbie his work address, he told him to go back to the street where he had seen the bowling balls.

The cabbie looked like he was from somewhere in the Middle East. He had curly hair and obsidian eyes. There was a TV turned on in the front seat, and he kept looking down at it as he drove.

When they reached the street, Gerald was just in time to see the man with the truck throw in the last of the balls. The man hopped onto the back of the truck again, and knocked twice on its side, and then the truck headed off.

The cabbie didn't make any comment when Gerald told him to follow it. He just nodded. Soon they were heading west on one of the freeways. Gerald sat with his arms on the front seat, looking anxiously at the truck in front of them.

As they drove along, the cabbie switched off the volume of the TV.

"Are you from out of town?" the cabbie said with a heavy accent.

"Why do you ask that?" Gerald said.

The man laughed and turned around.

"No, in my estimation, you're from the city," he said. "I can tell now. People from the city always want to know first why you want to know."

Gerald was silent. The truck with the bowling balls had passed another car, and he couldn't see it anymore. "Don't lose it," he told the cabbie.

The man laughed again and said, "Don't you worry, sir." He added after a pause, "In my estimation, you've lived here quite some years. Maybe seven years. I can tell that because I'm very perceptive."

"I've only been here three years," said Gerald. The meter was already running high, as though he'd been riding in this cab for seven years.

"You must learn fast," said the man in an impressed tone. "Like me. I've only been in this country three weeks. When I first arrived here, I had a hundred and fifty dollars. I gave it to a friend of a friend and the next day I had this cab to drive around. I find this fact utterly amazing."

The driver seemed sort of crass to Gerald, and he wasn't sure he liked him, but he was glad that the man was talkative. Gerald felt like he was getting too wrapped up in himself. On the other hand, he couldn't care less about the man's immigrant adventures.

"What do you think about bowling balls?" Gerald said.

"Why do you want to know?" the cabbie said quickly, and then he laughed. "I know nothing about bowling balls," he went on. "I have no feelings for them. In fact I have never heard of them before now. But because I am so perceptive, I know that they must have a practical purpose. Perhaps when I have some money, I will choose to invest in them."

"You don't invest in bowling balls," said Gerald. "You throw them. You knock down pins with them. It's a very simple game with a clear-cut goal. There's nothing very important about bowling balls at all."

"Then thank you for warning me," said the cabbie. "I will be sure not to bother with them. It's true that we must not waste our time with unimportant things. In my room, I have a list of unimportant things that is taped to my wall. I already have over fifteen hundred things on the list and I have memorized them all. Learning what to ignore has made me perceptive."

After some time the truck left the freeway and turned off into an industrial area. Most of the buildings were warehouses, huge things with broken windows and gang signs scribbled on their walls. The truck pulled into a small alley between two of these buildings and disappeared.

Gerald had never seen this part of the city and he felt lost as the cab pulled up to the warehouse. But he believed he had made the right decision to follow this truck and not go to work. Though he had never been looking for anything in particular, his life had been littered with clues, as if he was on some kind of treasure hunt. As he sat in the back seat of the cab with the meter still running, he realized something he had perhaps always known. It came down to this: The clues were different for him. The things he found on the street. The things he saw as he walked along. The reason he never drove. He didn't want everything to add up neatly. He didn't want to become like the elder Gerald Kemp or this cabbie with his list of unimportant things. He didn't mind moving haphazardly from one clue to the next. His only small hope was that the things he saw and did would eventually lead somewhere. He saw himself climbing a hill of coincidences, reaching some peak, looking down, and, at the very least, knowing where he'd come from.

The meter on the cab now read $17.10, and Gerald reached for the muddy twenty-dollar bill in his wallet. Then he fished in his pocket, pulled a dime out, and realized it was the same one he'd found that morning. He laughed and handed the money over to the man, saying, "My advice is that you forget everything you've memorized. Otherwise you'll have a very narrow life. You might know where you're going, but you'll never find money on the sidewalk."

The man nodded and smiled and said thank you, but then he looked at Gerald strangely. For a moment Gerald imagined the man adding him to his list.

"Would you like me to wait, sir?" the man said, but Gerald felt as perceptive as the cabbie and saw that the man didn't want to wait around.

After the cab left, Gerald heard a rolling and crashing sound from the building. He assumed that men were unloading the balls back there somewhere. Even from a distance it was the most irritating and mindless noise he'd ever heard, like the balls were rolling steadily across metal, like a hundred jackhammers pounding the ground together. But even worse than that.

Clues

Eventually the noise stopped. The truck started up again and rumbled as it made its way back down the alley. Before the truck reached the road, Gerald walked towards the entrance of the building.

The warehouse was set back from the street behind a wide lot of cracked concrete. The building itself took up about a block. Hundreds of small windows dotted its walls, and most were broken. As he approached the building, he couldn't walk a step without crunching glass beneath his feet.

As the truck neared him, he ran for the chained and bolted entrance, which was set in a shadowed alcove. He stayed there until the truck had gone away.

Something shone among the glass shards. A penny. He put it in his pocket, and felt lucky again.

He looked for a company name or some other clue, but the only thing around was an old fallout shelter sign, its orange triangle set against the brick of the building.

He walked around to the alley and headed towards the back of the building. There was another warehouse on the other side, and the alley he walked through was narrow and unevenly paved, with shallow depressions where water had collected. The walls gave off a faint smell of oil, and both buildings had gang signs on them: a crown and "Latin Kings" written in fake Old English lettering. Over the King signs, the Gaylords had written their name in stark black scrawls. Higher up, the broken windows on both buildings were interspersed with heavy panes of block glass the vandals had been unable to break.

At the back of the building was a loading dock with corrugated metal doors. The loading dock was large and deserted. If he ran into someone, he didn't know what he'd tell them, maybe that he'd gotten lost. "Is Iowa around here somewhere?" he imagined himself saying to some dockworker. He saw himself getting beat up by a crowd who appeared from nowhere: the Latin Kings, the Gaylords, the cops, his family. You're not supposed to be back here. You belong at work, in Iowa, anywhere you don't want to go.

After a while, he stopped and stood still. There was no one else around, and soon he even stopped worrying that someone would catch him. He knew for certain that he had been led here, and that eventually he'd find an entrance, and that inside he'd discover why all those people had been acting so strangely. He looked up at the building, around at its sides, and then down towards the ground. He walked slowly towards a door set into the wall.

The door opened easily. He was in an empty hall with sunlight making streaks on the floor. The hall looked hundreds of yards long, and he walked towards the other side. As he was making his way through the room, he realized he had made a mistake, that maybe he shouldn't have come here by himself. He could have taken the foreign cabbie. Or a friend or even a total stranger. Somehow he would have convinced them that it was important. Without anyone else, he wasn't proving anything, and for the first time he felt a deep and lonely doubt about himself.

But he kept going. The light dwindled as he went farther into the hall. The thick squares of block glass barely allowed any light through. He started talking to himself to keep from becoming overwhelmed by the emptiness. He imagined someone coming out of the shadows towards him, some baritone-voiced figure who would explain all his mysteries.

"Ah, so we meet at last."

"Yes, I knew you would come."

Clues

Nothing like that happened. He didn't really expect it, and yet he couldn't walk another step without some further clue to show him he was headed in the right direction.

He stubbed his toe. He jumped back as though he'd been bitten and grabbed his foot. He heard something roll away from him, and then saw it. A bowling ball.

He felt around, eyes still adjusting to the dim light. He found the ball and reached out, but it was still rolling slowly and moved away just beyond his grasp.

As he reached for it again, he stumbled on something else and fell to the ground. Bowling balls were scattered all over.

He started to rise, but then he heard something beside him. The noise grew in volume. It sounded like a rack of dishes shaking in some giant dishwasher, or a million people grinding their teeth together at once.

In front and above him was a huge mountain of bowling balls, black and dull, hundreds deep and thousands wide, in a pile going all the way up to the ceiling. He had never seen anything so massive and confusing as this. It was simply horrible, and was like nothing he'd ever expected.

The mountain roiled and made an even more startling noise as it shifted like a wave about to break. He closed his eyes and waited for the mountain to come over him.

What would it sound like back in his own neighborhood? He saw the black squirrel dropping a nut from a tree. This is how it would sound, but not even that loud. It would be the tiniest noise, so small you'd never notice.

43

Riding the
Whip

The night before my sister died a friend of my parents, Natalie Ganzer, took me and her niece to a carnival. I couldn't stand Natalie, but I fell in love with the niece, a girl about fifteen named Rita. On the ferris wheel Rita grabbed my hand. On any other ride I would have thought she was only frightened and wanted security. But this ferris wheel was so tame and small. There was nothing to be afraid of at fifty feet.

When we got down and the man let us out of the basket, I kept hold of Rita's hand, and she didn't seem to mind.

"Oh, I'm so glad you children are enjoying the evening," said Natalie. "It's so festive. There's nothing like a carnival, is there?"

Normally I would have minded being called a child, but not tonight. Things were improving. There was nothing to worry about, my mother had told me over the phone earlier that evening. Yes, Julie had done a stupid thing, but only to get attention.

Still, something was wrong, something bugged me about that night, where I was, the carnival and its sounds. I was having too much fun and I knew I shouldn't be. Already I had won a stuffed animal from one of the booths and given it to Rita. And usually I got nauseated on rides, but tonight they just made me laugh. Red neon swirled around on the rides, and barkers yelled at us on the fairway. Popguns blew holes in targets, and there were so many people screaming and laughing beside us that I could hardly take it in. I just stood there feeling everyone else's fun moving through me, and I could hardly hear what Rita and Natalie were saying. "Come on, Jay," shouted Rita. My hand was being tugged. "Let's ride the Whip." The whip. That didn't make any sense to me. A whip wasn't something you rode. It was something to hurt you, something from movies that came down hard on prisoners' backs and left them scarred.

"You can't ride a whip," I shouted to her over the noise.

She laughed and said, "Why not? Don't be scared. You won't get sick, I promise."

"Aren't you having fun, Jay?" Natalie said. "Your parents want you to have fun, and I'm sure that's what Julie wants too."

I didn't answer, though I was having fun. Things seemed brighter and louder than a moment before. I could even hear a girl on the ferris wheel say to someone, "You're cute, did you know that?" One carny in his booth stood out like a detail in a giant painting. He held a bunch of strings in his hand. The strings led to some stuffed animals. "Everyone's a winner," he said.

The carnival was just a painting, a bunch of petals in a bowl, which made me think of Julie. She was an artist and painted still lifes mostly, but she didn't think she was any good. My parents had discouraged her, but I bought a large painting of hers once with some paper money I cut from a notebook. A week before the carnival she came into my room and slashed the painting to bits. "She's not herself," my mother told me. "You know she loves you."

Now we stood at the gates of the Whip. Rita gave her stuffed animal to Natalie, who held it by the paw as though it were a new ward of hers. The man strapped us into our seat and Rita said to me, "You're so quiet. Aren't you having fun?"

"Sure," I said. "Doesn't it look like it?"

"Your sister's crazy, isn't she?" said Rita. "I mean, doing what she did."

I knew I shouldn't answer her, that I should step out of the ride and go home.

"She just sees things differently," I said.

"What do you mean?" Rita said. She was looking at me strangely, as though maybe I saw things differently too. I didn't want to see differently. I didn't want to become like my sister.

"Sure she's crazy," I said. "I don't even care what happens to her."

Then the ride started up, and we laughed and screamed. We moved like we weren't people anymore, but electrical currents charging from different sources.

In the middle of the ride something grazed my head. A metal bar hung loose along one of the turns and each time we whipped around it, the bar touched me. The metal barely hit me, but going so fast it felt like being knocked with a sandbag. It didn't hit anyone else, just me, and I tried several times to get out of the way, but I was strapped in, and there was no way to avoid it.

At the end of the ride I was completely punch drunk, and I could barely speak. Rita, who mistook my expression for one of pleasure, led me over to Natalie.

"That was fun," said Rita. "Let's go on the Cat and Mouse now."

Riding the Whip

My vision was blurry, and my legs were wobbling a bit. "I want to go on the Whip again," I said.

Natalie and Rita looked at each other. Natalie reached out towards my head, and I pulled back from her touch. "You're *bleeding*, Jay," she said. Her hand stayed in midair, and she looked at me as though she were someone in a gallery trying to get a better perspective on a curious painting.

I broke away from them into the crowd and made my way back to the Whip. After paying the man, I found the same seat. I knew which one it was because it was more beat up than the rest, with several gashes in the cushion, as though someone had taken a long knife and scarred it that way on purpose.

Looking for Kin

For three weeks I was scared of the mill. I thought the machines were out to get me. I thought the men were out to get me. I saw the furnaces, the scrap trains, and the lathes as personal threats, even though I rarely came in contact with them. I worked outside as a dock foreman, a job my Uncle Ted arranged for me, and one that required little experience, merely the ability to keep people moving.

After my initial fright, I settled into the place. No longer did I think I'd wind up as part of some farmer's tractor by the end of the summer. And I convinced myself that I'd cut my ties with the college world, at least for now. After all, I had broken up with my girlfriend Delores over this job. She wanted me to spend the summer with her family in Colorado and couldn't understand why I'd rather work in Gary, Indiana.

I tried to be honest with her, which was the wrong approach. I said, "Delores, you told me once that your name means sadness in Spanish, and basically I think you're a nice person, though you make me pretty sad. This doesn't mean that things are over between us. I just think I should be frank and tell you what's wrong with you. Then you can tell me what's wrong with me, and maybe after that we'll become closer."

48

Looking for Kin

To Delores's credit, she didn't even reply. She just walked out of my room. I thought she was immature and decided I didn't need her anyway. But when I saw her the next night at a roof party in the arms of Wild Bill, a thirty-year-old vet who spent all his time playing euchre and simulated war games, I was upset she'd throw me over for such a loser.

So I plunged myself into the real world of the iron mill. Most of the men there stayed private, and for a while this was all right with me. The mill employed upwards of two thousand men, and guys showed up and disappeared before you even knew their names. There was a guy who started working one night and kept on for three weeks with hardly a break. He would have worked continuously, but the mill shuts down at seven every morning so the maintenance men can fix the bearings on all the machines and keep the place running. It turned out this guy was a murderer. He'd hacked up his brother-in-law for having incest with his wife. I happened to be working alongside him the night the cops came to get him.

The two cops wandered aimlessly around the docks for a while, playing with the guy before they moved in. We both saw them coming. I had just smoked a joint. I still had half an ounce in my pocket, and I naturally thought they were coming for me, not knowing this other guy's record. As the cops approached, both this murderer and I began to do our work very slowly.

You can't escape the noise of the mill. Even outside, the crashing of the scrap metal deafens you. But after you've worked there awhile, you come to recognize and be wary of any foreign sound. So everyone within earshot of those cops' boots, clapping like war drums on the dock, stopped work and stood at the edge of our confrontation.

49

My murderous partner and I were unloading crates of chemicals. Under the mercury lights his face was tense and sleepworn; his body moving mechanically.

Only when the cops were right beside us did we stop moving. I stabbed my hand into my pocket, clenched the bag of pot, and prepared to chuck it as far as I could. One of the cops made a motion towards me, meaning I should stand aside, but which I interpreted as "We got you and your Commie dope ring now, buster."

I thought they might be easier on me in the long run if I admitted my crime. I pulled the bag of pot from my pocket and tried to hand it to the cop. "Here's what you're looking for," I said.

The cop's concentration was broken for a moment, and he looked from the pot to me in astonishment. So my partner made a break for it, but was tackled immediately by the other cop.

As soon as I saw my mistake, I looked around to see if any of my fellow workers had seen what I had done. But no one was paying any attention to me.

The murderer started yelling, "You got me wrong. I ain't done nothing." And then he started calling to me for help, even though the cuffs were already on him, and there was nothing I could do. It was the first time he ever talked to me. He even used my name. "Greg, tell them they wrong. Go on, tell them."

I forgot my previous foolishness and joined a semi-circle of men looking at the cops as though *they* were the ones who'd committed the crime. But there was nothing we could do, and so we just stood there.

Then a man I knew as Johnny Mitro walked up to the cops and said, "What you jokers doin' here? What you got on my man Samuel?"

"Move your ass," said one of the cops, and shoved

Looking for Kin

Johnny. He didn't budge. He had his legs apart, and he kept his balance even though the cop had pushed him hard.

Johnny was tall and lanky. He didn't look imposing, but cool. He wore jeans and a workshirt like the rest of us, but had his shirt half unbuttoned and a crucifix dangling from his neck. "You a blivit, man," Johnny said to the cop, and the men around me laughed. Blivit was the mill term for ten pounds of shit crammed in a five-pound bag. But the cop didn't know that. "I ask you a simple question," he continued. "What you got on this man?"

The cop looked like he was ready to bust Johnny, but some other guys in the crowd joined in a chorus, saying, "Yeah, what he do?" These guys must have looked mean to the cop's partner, an old guy who seemed ready to retire at that moment. He told us in simple, condescending terms what Samuel was wanted for. Now that we knew, we felt even worse. We didn't care what the man had done. The cops had invaded, humiliated him, and given away his secret.

After the cops took their man away, the other men made a hero out of Johnny and everyone gathered around each other like they were kin. If they didn't know someone's name they made one up. I couldn't get them back to work. I had no real power over them anyway. They did their work when they wanted and because they wanted. They never paid me much attention, but until that moment I hadn't minded too much. I was still upset about Delores. After all, I had just been honest with her, and I couldn't see anything wrong with that. So at the mill I had imposed silence on myself like a lot of my co-workers.

A group of men surrounded Johnny, listening to him recount his story, even though they had all wit-

51

nessed it. Even the hard-asses seemed to admire Johnny, especially his buddy Dewitt, who stood beside him. Johnny and Dewitt were the biggest studs in the mill. They were legendary. Though Dewitt rarely talked, Johnny spent most of his time trying to keep up with his image. If the mill had paid Johnny for breaks, he would have made a fortune. He hardly lifted a finger, but I never bothered him because I was scared of Dewitt. Dewitt was older than Johnny, maybe late thirties. It wasn't his size that scared everyone. He never sneered, bared his teeth, or anything like that. In other circumstances, he could have been a middle-aged businessman, with his soft, almost feminine mouth and his bald head. But he wasn't a businessman. He had a prison record and was too distant for anyone to get to know. No one knew why he had gone to prison. Some people said it was a stolen car scam. Others swore he had crippled some homosexual who'd made a pass at him.

The latter wasn't hard to believe. If you touched him, he'd kill you. He didn't want anyone touching him, except for Johnny, who had earned the right. Even Johnny could only touch him for a moment, like when he'd slap Dewitt's shoulder and say, "Hey man, check this out." If anyone else touched Dewitt, even brushed against his arm, he'd grab the guy and say, "What kind of woman is you anyhow?"

I tried now to join the conversation but no one would let me. Each time I said something, there would be a silence, and then they'd continue as though I wasn't there. I thought maybe they blamed me for the cops taking that man away. Then I realized that I was an outsider just like the cops, and so I left them.

After this, I started to realize I was accepted only as long as I didn't participate in the storytelling at the mill.

Looking for Kin

The men who told these stories were, in all cases, the studs. I wanted to be a stud too, and started affecting some of their mannerisms. I strutted around the docks, shoulders loose, arms flip-flopping at my sides, my head bobbing up and down. I wanted to be a stud, because I saw only studs and blivits around me. On the one hand, there was Wild Bill, a major blivit who did nothing but play euchre and simulated war games. Yet somehow he wound up with Delores, an intelligent woman, a French Civilization major. On the other hand, there were the studs like Johnny Mitro, men who were cool, shrewd, and worldly. The studs had it all to begin with, and they never lost it.

The week before I was supposed to return to school we had a rush order from International Harvester. Everyone was working overtime and so we were all tired and irritable that week. One night I passed a pile of crates and an idle forklift with its motor still on. If I wanted to return next summer, I couldn't let management see this. So I searched for and found those responsible: Dewitt, Johnny, and another man named Floyd August. They had cleared out a space in the middle of the crates and were sitting around smoking a joint and swapping stories.

After scrambling over a few crates to reach the three men, I went into my stud foreman act. I let my shoulders droop, scratched my ear, and bobbed my head up and down.

"You guys should be working," I said, but they couldn't hear me over the noise. Even though we were outside, the clank of the magnetic crane we called the shitworker, which unloaded scrap metal from the trains, echoed around us. That sound was combined with the sounds of the lathes, the converters, and all the other machines of the mill. That's why a lot of deaf

53

people worked there. They hadn't gone deaf from the noise. Most of them had been born deaf and worked at the mill because the noise didn't bother them.

I went right up to the three of them, even though I was wary of Dewitt.

"Hey, Joe Cool," said Johnny. "What you floppin' about like that for? Make you look like some shake and bake chicken."

Floyd and Johnny laughed. Dewitt stood up and looked down at me like I was some kind of animal he'd never seen before.

"Okay, guys," I said. "Fun's over. Get back to work."

"College boy say get back to work," said Johnny.

"Look, I don't want to have to dock anyone," I said.

Johnny just smiled, stood up next to Dewitt, who towered over me, and put his arm around my shoulder. "Now, Greg," he said. "Let's talk this thing through. I mean man to man. That's what you is, ain't it?"

"Don't know," said Floyd. "Maybe we better check him out. Bend over, Greg, and let's see."

"Hush, Floyd," said Johnny. "Can't you see I'm talking to my man Greg?"

This guy, Floyd, bothered me. He was a short, stocky man with a friendly face who had worked in the mill for twenty years. When I talked to him alone, he'd hang on my every breath, but as soon as someone else came along his eyes would wander back and forth, and he'd get a stupid grin on his face like I was a joke he couldn't avoid. I never heard him say anything bad about me, but I couldn't stand him all the same. At least Johnny taunted me outright. I could deal with Johnny because he didn't really mean the things he said. He tested people with his taunts and tried to get a rise from everyone except for Dewitt, who didn't need testing.

Floyd, on the other hand, was friendly as long as it suited him. Then he'd turn on you.

"I really think I'm going to have to dock you guys," I said, straining to keep some authority in my voice.

Dewitt had been staring at me for some time. He took a step towards me without altering his fix. But then his eyes clasped tight like he couldn't stand the sight of me a moment longer, and he sneezed. Johnny and Floyd laughed because it looked like Dewitt was allergic to me. I didn't think this was funny. I hadn't made him sneeze. It was the black sand that's used in making grey iron, the type made at our mill. This sand, like the noise, gets all over the mill, inside and out. The sand settles in your pores, cakes your nose, and when you swallow it feels like chicken beaks and feathers going down your throat.

Dewitt thought they were laughing at him. "I got sand up my nose," he said, sniffing once and then resuming his former attitude of disdain.

"Now come on," I said. "Break it up. We're working on a deadline."

Johnny, his arm still around my shoulder, took a drag on his roach and said, "Hey man, what you so bothered about? We ain't done nothin' and you ain't gonna dock us, cause if you do, my man Dewitt's gonna slap you around like a redheaded stepchild. Then you be so ugly they not gonna let you back into college. They say, 'Who this ugly dude come down from Gary? Scat mother, you too *ugly* to go to school.' "

"Are you threatening me?" I asked.

"Am I threatenin' *you*. Man, you is one dumb motherfucker. Who threatenin' who anyhow? We just tokin' some ganja, takin' a break."

"Yeah," said Floyd. "We just talking bout how cool the foreman is."

Johnny handed the roach to Floyd. Then he unbuttoned his shirt pocket and withdrew another joint, a fat one. He lit it, inhaled deeply, and handed it to me. "Go ahead. Take a little of this and loosen your ass up."

I took the joint and stared at it. Then I looked at Dewitt. He was watching me like I was a laboratory rat, and he was a scientist trying to prove some awful theory by me. I couldn't figure out what he wanted me to do. On the one hand, he probably wanted me to leave. But if I refused the pot, I'd be insulting them, maybe even challenging them further. So I took a drag. What the hell. The other men could do their work without me anyway. This was my last week, and all summer I'd wanted to be in with these people. I could tell Johnny liked me. I noticed the way he glanced at me from time to time. As though I was his baby brother, which was the same way Dewitt glanced at him.

We started telling stories, about women of course. Floyd started with one about a wild night of whoring in Puerto Rico, when he was in the merchant marines.

"Every one of them bitches in bed with me," Floyd said, "and them sailors outside pounding on the door, saying, 'Let us have our turn, man.' So I leaves it up to the bitches, and they say, 'No, Floyd honey. We just fine where we is.'"

I didn't believe him for a moment. "That's physically impossible," I said. "You'd be too tired."

Floyd looked hurt that I'd doubt him, but then he said, "Tired? Shit. The bitches was pulling on my arm, *begging* me to stay."

Throughout Floyd's story, Dewitt had kept a watchful eye on me, like some kind of judge. After the story was done, Dewitt smiled and nodded.

Johnny, on the other hand, seemed amused by my

reactions, and every once in a while he'd look at me and say, "How bout that, Greg?"

Soon I started to loosen up. I was the highest of them all. Every other word I said was *motherfucker*. I was a cool dude. I worked in the mill, knew where the action was, knew the right people, knew what to say. I could get a woman, maybe ten. I'd sell ludes on the side, forget about college, buy a car just to wreck it, and cruise the lakeshore with my man Johnny Mitro.

Now I wanted to tell a story. It didn't even occur to me to make one up. I didn't know the rules, so I launched right into an account of my near seduction of a woman the year before, when I was still a virgin.

"What is you? Thirteen?" said Johnny. "You mean to say you never had tang til you was twenty?"

"Nineteen," I said, hunching my shoulders. "Yes, motherfucker," I continued. "Sad but motherfucking true. I almost motherfucked a year earlier though."

"Say what?" asked Johnny. "You did *what*?"

I guessed I was using the term a bit excessively and decided to drop it.

I told them about the girl I picked up at a dorm party. I lied to her. She was so gullible she believed all of my story. Or maybe she didn't. I said I had grown up in China, that my father was the American ambassador, and that I had returned to the U.S. to go to school. I wasn't used to American customs. Would she please show me some? I asked. I got her to leave the party with me. We took a walk, holding hands. We were both pretty drunk, and I didn't even care if she was attractive, I was so absorbed in the fact I was picking up a woman. We stopped in front of the president's mansion.

"The president's mansion?" Floyd asked at this point. "Where was you anyhow?"

"Floyd, you is a real blivit," said Johnny. "Can't you see the man's telling a story? It don't matter where he was."

So I continued, trying to tell my story like a stud would in present tense and ungrammatically. As soon as I started, Dewitt turned his head away like he was ashamed, but Johnny and Floyd seemed to get a kick out of this.

"There's this tree there," I said. "We sit down out of view and I kisses her. Soon I'm undressing her, but I can't get her panties down . . . none. All I get is to feel her up some."

"Shit, Greg," said Johnny, laughing. "You talk to your mama like that? You sound like a robot."

"So what you do after you feel up her some?" asked Floyd, holding his hands by his chest and mechanically squeezing a pair of invisible tits.

"I didn't do anything, because she smiled at me and said, 'Maybe we shouldn't do this. I don't know you. I like to know people for two weeks before I go to bed with them. You might have some kind of disease.' "

"You might have some kind of disease?" yelled Johnny. "Shit, we all got disease. It's called tang fever."

Johnny and Floyd laughed at me again. Dewitt just looked at me accusingly and said, "How she gonna know you got some disease after two weeks if you ain't fucked her?"

"I don't know. You'll have to ask her," I said, barely paying attention to him. I was caught up in my story. I had never told it before because it made me look bad. But I wanted these people, especially Johnny, to allow me to look bad.

"But wait," I continued. "I'm coming to the worst part. After she wouldn't screw me, I started shivering. I couldn't stop, and she was just lying back, smiling at me. I had to run home and get away. I never saw her again, but now I think she planned it all. I think she knew the story I was telling was a lie, and she was just getting revenge on me."

"Man, that sad," said Floyd. "Why you tell a story like that?"

"Hell, we're all friends, aren't we?" I said.

Dewitt shook his ponderous head back and forth as though he was the first person to arrive at the scene of some horrible accident, and said, "Like shit."

Johnny was looking at Dewitt like he was trying to figure him out but addressed Floyd. "Floyd, you just one low-rent motherfucker. The man right. We all friends."

"What about you, Dewitt?" I said, trying to break some of the tension. "Did anything ever go wrong between you and a woman?"

"Nothing ever gone wrong with me, nothing but prison."

"No, nothing gone wrong with him," said Johnny. "Man, I had things gone wrong," he continued, and started to tell his own story.

"Every night," he said, "me and my man Dewitt over here goes cruising for action down by the lake. You get some fine-looking pie down there. We never gone home without a piece yet, ain't that right, Dewitt?" Dewitt didn't answer.

"One night, Dewitt has to stay overtime, so I goes cruising alone. In no time I see this fancy bitch, I mean sugar, and she comes slinking up to my windshield."

Dewitt looked at Johnny reproachfully, as though he knew what he was going to say, but didn't want him to say it. Throughout Johnny's story, Dewitt stared him down with a look of betrayal. Johnny hardly seemed to notice. In fact, Johnny only acknowledged him once, just long enough to give him a fiery look in return, and then continued.

"The bitch got tight pants, tight top, custom-built tits, and a bucket seat. So I say, 'Oh Mama, want to come for a ride in Daddy's car?' And she just nods and gets in. Man, she into my pants before we halfway home."

"Man, how you get so lucky, an ugly nigger like you?" said Floyd.

"Just a stud, I guess," I said.

Johnny smiled at me without much conviction.

Dewitt bunched his fists at his sides, moved close to Johnny, did everything he could but nudge him.

Floyd and I were silent, both of us feeling awkward and unsure of what was going on. Behind me, I could hear the shitworker unloading scrap. By this time we were all gritty with sand, ugly and feeling miserable.

"At my place," Johnny continued, "we toke some ganja, drink a brew, and all the time she just smile and stays pretty. So I say, 'Woman, you pass the test,' but when I reach down to her nest I grab this thing. 'Man,' I said. 'You got a pecker.' "

Johnny stretched out his arms. "The motherfucker had a pecker this long. And then I look over at the motherfucker's purse and I see a knife as long as his pecker. 'Don't make no difference to me,' say the bitch, 'and it better make no difference to you.' "

"So what did you do?" I said.

"What you think I done? I fucked the son of a bitch."

Dewitt turned on Johnny furiously. "Like shit you did. Why you lie like that?"

"That's what happened," said Johnny.

"You fucked him? That's what you tellin' this college boy?"

"Hey," said Johnny. "You heard the man. We all friends."

60

Looking for Kin

Dewitt looked confused for a moment. "You know what you saying?"

"You hear what I say," said Johnny defiantly. He laughed, trying to get hold of the situation. "Sure I fucked him. I fuck anything. I'll fuck your bow-legged dog if you got a knife long as your pecker."

Dewitt looked at me like he wished I would disappear, but seeing I wouldn't, he said to Johnny, "I known you. Now you say you a queer? A screamer? Man, you disgusting."

Floyd and I were transfixed. Dewitt looked ready to punch Johnny, but then he whirled around, scrambled over the crates, and was gone. I was sure this was all an act. I knew Dewitt had heard the story before. It was that last look he gave Johnny.

Johnny just stood there, exhausted, saying nothing, as though he had said the world.

Now I was important to them, even dangerous, because I had heard one of them shamed. I was even more dangerous than Floyd, who was certain to tell the other workers what had happened.

I looked at Johnny, who seemed shocked at what he had said. Floyd walked soberly away soon after Dewitt, saying, "See you 'round, man."

I couldn't think of anything to say but, "We'd better get back to work."

Johnny didn't answer, and so I left him, too. When I looked back I saw an unfamiliar and ordinary man lighting a joint inside a circle of crates. I still could have docked him. I could have done any number of things. But by now I was too far away to smell it, and the gritty rush of smoke through Johnny's lungs was drowned out by the mill's perpetual clamor.

A week later I left the mill and returned to school. I felt too ugly to go anywhere else.

Dropping
the Baby

Harry dropped the baby head first on the linoleum kitchen floor.

"Harry! That's my only baby," Louise shouted. "How could you be so clumsy?"

Harry bent to pick up the pieces, looked up at her guiltily, and said, "Sorry, my mistake."

Luckily it was all a dream, and Louise woke up.

She hurried into the kitchen, where Harry was burning the toast. He wore his cotton bathrobe with a silk sash tied around the waist. He was bent over the toaster. The smoke from the toast and the smoke from his morning cigar rose up around his head. The smoke looked like it was coming from his ears, like he was some kind of crazy cartoon character who had just swallowed a bomb.

"Harry," said Louise. "You've got to stop doing this to me. You're driving me crazy."

Harry turned around, took the cigar out of his mouth, and laid it across the top of the toaster. He opened his arms and walked towards Louise. He looked like a cross between a gunslinger showing he was unarmed and the Pope giving benediction.

"Hey, sorry about the toast," he said, grabbing her shoulders and rubbing his nose in her neck. "I was trying to surprise you again."

Dropping the Baby

"Do me a favor. No more surprises. Anyway, I meant the baby. You keep dropping the goddamn baby."

"Hey come on," said Harry, taking his nose from her neck, and leading her to the kitchen table. "Calm down, huh? You certainly can't keep blaming me for this baby stuff. It's *your* dream."

"I know, I know," said Louise, taking a seat.

Instead of joining her, Harry walked to the kitchen window and opened it. The smoke started to clear.

"I don't know what it is with this dream," said Louise, putting a hand through her hair and tugging at a few strands.

"I'll tell you what it is," said Harry, going to the stove and flipping the pancakes in a skillet. "It's irrational, that's what it is."

"Don't be angry with me," said Louise. "I can't help it if you keep dropping the baby."

Harry turned around and motioned to her with the spatula. He had fat cheeks and a high forehead which Louise knew people used to think was a sure sign of intelligence. His eyes were clear and blue. "I haven't dropped any baby," he said. "Will you please forget it? It doesn't mean anything."

"It has to mean something," she said, "or I wouldn't keep having the dream. I walk into the kitchen and you're standing there holding the baby like a jackhammer. Then when you see me walk in, you just drop it on the floor."

Harry picked up his cigar from the toaster and took a puff, but it had gone out. "Look," he said. "You don't have to keep telling me about the dream. I know it by heart already. If you don't stop it, I'm going to start dreaming about this baby. You tell a person something long enough and they start to believe it." He withdrew a

63

pack of matches from his bathrobe pocket and relit the cigar.

"What does this alleged baby look like?" he said.

"A mushroom."

"A mushroom? Then it's a mushroom dream, not a baby dream."

"No, it's a baby dream," said Louise. "It's just that it's got a big head like a mushroom. Maybe it's sexual."

"Why?" Harry said. "Is there something wrong with me?"

"No, you're perfect," said Louise.

"Then why did you say there was something wrong with me sexually?"

"I didn't say something was wrong with you. Don't put words in my mouth."

"Then don't dream I'm a baby killer," said Harry, removing a loaf of bread from the refrigerator. He unwrapped the twist cord and took out two slices. Then he replaced the burnt slices in the toaster with the new bread. He tossed the burnt toast in the trash.

"We need a new toaster," he said. "You promised me a new toaster."

"There's nothing wrong with the toaster," said Louise.

Harry was silent.

"Maybe it's an abortion dream," said Louise. "Maybe I think you don't love me enough to want me to have a baby. What do you think about that, Harry?"

"A baby wouldn't be a good idea right now," he said.

"I wasn't suggesting one. I don't even want one. But why not? Why don't you think it would be a good idea? I'm just interested, that's all."

"You know why," he said, returning to the stove and giving the pancakes another flip. "Don't insult me."

64

"Don't get upset," said Louise. "I was just curious, that's all."

Louise looked at the paunch Harry was developing. He was drinking too much beer. Everyday when she returned home from work, she and Harry had a couple of beers. But Harry always drank at least another six pack before she got home.

She didn't even know what he did all day. The only signs that he even existed were the cigar butts in the ashtray and the empty beer cans by the TV.

Maybe he watched "General Hospital." Maybe he tried on her underwear. She thought of him dancing around the house in a slip, the mushroom baby tucked under his arm.

The week before she had returned home early and caught him masturbating in bed. He didn't even look embarrassed when he opened his eyes and saw her standing in front of him. He just closed his eyes again and said, "You're home early."

"Who are you thinking of?" she said.

"You," he said, gathering his bathrobe around him.

No, it would be impossible for them to have a baby now, not until Harry got a job.

The thought of a baby had always frightened her. She remembered when she was thirteen and was convinced she was pregnant, even though she hadn't even kissed a boy before. She didn't even know how she had got the notion in her head. One day she just decided she was pregnant, and for four months she thought her stomach was growing. She was terrified that her mother would find out. She even told her best friend at school that she needed an abortion. Finally she told her mother what she suspected. Her mother calmly sat her down and explained that she couldn't have a baby without a man.

"Years from now," she told Louise, "when you're grown up and married, your husband will decide to have a baby, and lickety-split, you'll have a baby."

"*D*o you want to get pregnant?" Harry said.

"You're right," said Louise. "We should wait. Is the coffee done? I should get going soon."

Harry grabbed the Mr. Coffee pot. He took a cup from the kitchen sink and set it in front of her.

He dipped the coffee pot, and a stream of coffee poured onto the table, missing the cup completely. Before Louise could move, half the coffee was in her lap.

She jumped up, wiping the spill with her hand. "You're so damn clumsy," she said. "Don't you have any depth perception?"

"I'm sorry," he said and ran to the sink for a towel. As he was running back with the towel in hand, his bathrobe fell open.

"Does spilling coffee on your wife turn you on?" she said.

"Damn it, I'm sorry," he said. "I'm just nervous. Can't you give me a break?"

Harry wiped the table off first, and then started to wipe his wife's crotch with the soaking rag.

Louise jumped away from him. "Harry. What are you doing? Look what you've done. You've made it worse. This will never come off."

"I'm sorry," he said, running again for the sink. "I'll get some water."

"No," said Louise. "Don't. Don't come near me," and she sank into her chair. "Just get me some pancakes."

66

"Okay," he said. "Look, don't worry. These will be great. Real delights. But they're not quite done yet."

Harry grabbed the spatula and flipped a pancake into the air. The pancake looped once and fell next to Louise's feet.

It happened so suddenly that Louise screamed when it hit the ground. She covered her face with her hands and felt tears coming to her eyes.

"God, Harry," she said. "What have I done that makes you hate me so much?"

"I don't hate you," said Harry. He knelt beside her and picked up the pancake. He held it in his hand like a Bible and said, "I love you. I swear."

She ran a hand through his hair. "Then Harry," she said, "do one thing for me."

"Anything," he said, grabbing her hands, though he still held the pancake.

"Give me a baby."

Before he had a chance to reply, she bent towards him and pushed him onto the linoleum floor. He looked stunned. She rolled him on top of her and opened her bathrobe.

Lying on her back, she felt totally absent. She looked up at the kitchen light and saw the shadows of bugs trapped in the shade. She smelled the toast burning. She saw the smoke rising from the ashtray. She imagined the other pancakes in the skillet, blackened and disgusting.

She knew she would leave him before he had a chance to do anything rash.

Polish
Luggage

❦

This might sound terrible, but I almost didn't come here today. I'm too independent, and Mother had to beg me to attend. Was I trying to punish her? she said. Did I want to make her an emotional cripple? Daddy did a good enough job of that, though I didn't tell her so. It's not that I'm callous. I just don't believe in these ceremonies and rituals that mark every significant passage in our lives. But Mother is so sentimental. She's planned the whole day as a near replica of her first date with Daddy. The guests are all assembled in the living room, drinking J&B and listening dutifully to the song that my parents heard that night. Personally I like the song, but Mother has it recorded on a tape loop. All we've been hearing for the last hour is:

> Here we are, out of cigarettes
> Holding hand in hand, see how late it gets
> Two sleepy people by dawn's early light
> Much too much in love to say goodnight

The plan calls next for a procession, stations of the cross fashion, from one memorable spot of their first date to another. First we'll drive past the Chinese restaurant where they had dinner that night, though it wasn't a

Chinese restaurant then but a fancy steakhouse with a seventeen-piece band. After that, we'll swing by the Parthenon Theater, and finally we'll trek out to the municipal airport where Daddy's ashes will be scattered from a plane high above the hill on which he and Mother watched the sunrise the next day. There's a dual beauty here, because Daddy was an airline pilot, though he would have preferred a 747 to a twin-prop Cessna. Rather than being dropped he would have liked the jet to explode him into Valhalla with his Viking ancestors.

But he's not complaining now. Mother has him in a bronze urn on a tray which she's passing around as though serving canapes.

My husband, Ross, comes up to me and says, "Your mother's slogged. You'd better do something with her before there's an accident."

"Why don't you go talk to her, Ross?" I say. "She'd like that, you know."

Ross pretends he hasn't heard and says, "Do I have something in my beard? I saw it drop in there."

Ross is carrying a picnic in his beard, which is nothing unusual. It's strange for him to be concerned, though. He's wearing a couple of different cheeses and some wheat cracker strands.

"You know I feel bad for Emily," he says after I've finished grooming him. "I'd rush over in a minute and talk to her if she wasn't your mother and I was a complete stranger. But all she ever talks about is how she and Lester were so disappointed when you broke off your engagement to Willis Tremont. And she still doesn't even know what I do for a living. She thinks a lobbyist is someone who passes out discount coupons at the shopping mall."

"Oh, Ross," I say and leave it at that. Not that I blame him, but at least Mother's always been more sympathetic to him than Daddy ever was. Five years ago when Ross and I married, Daddy's wedding gift was a pair of tickets to Miami. "From there, you can *swim* to Cuba," he told us.

Mother has cornered the funeral director on the living room couch. He's a glum, shriveled man with a goatee and an oversized suit. I'd always thought funeral directors were supposed to be kind and solicitous, even fawning. Leave it to Mother to get a rude mortician. He glances at his watch while she's talking, takes a handkerchief from his suit, and blows his nose.

"Lester hated small spaces," she tells the funeral director while holding the urn like a game show model displaying a set of crystal. "He always said the crew cabin made him claustrophobic. But he was such a tall man, nearly six four. Anyone under five ten he considered a dwarf."

The man gives her three jerky nods and turns away. Mother keeps gazing at him as though she expects him to talk to her, but he just scoots himself up in the couch and sips his drink. I agree Mother can be a clod sometimes, but that's still no reason for him to act so coldly, especially on a day like today.

"Mr. Grogan?" Mother says, tapping him on the shoulder. He turns around and gives her a sneer. He takes out his handkerchief again and sneezes loudly into it.

I take Mother under the arm and urge her out off the couch. "Why don't we lie down for a bit?" I suggest. "You're tired, Mother."

Mother blinks at me. She lets one of her hands dangle by her side and slowly strokes her leg, then grabs a swatch of her dress and bunches it in her fist. "We? We're not tired. We're not awfully tired," she says like a little girl trying to remember a nursery rhyme.

Polish Luggage

She looks up as though she doesn't know who I am, her eyes moving confusedly in her stricken face. She clutches Daddy's urn and opens her mouth as I lead her away from the couch. "How greatly," she tells me as though that's a sensible thing to say.

"Come on, Mother."

"How greatly," she says again.

She looks distressed so I nod and she nods back.

"Greatly," she says more calmly and looks at me as though I've understood.

When I return from Mother and Daddy's room, a few of the guests glance at me, and we exchange thin smiles.

My childhood is frozen in place in this living room. The house is dark, decorated in the baronial way Daddy liked: steins over the fireplace, heavy carved furniture, and rugs of maroon, purple, and gold.

We hardly spoke at all these last two years, though every time Mother called, I could hear him rasping on the extension. "Daddy, is that you?" I said several times, but he never answered and Mother always pretended he was taking a walk in the woods or napping on the sundeck. I visited a year ago when Daddy was worsening fast and Mother needed me around for support. The moment I walked in the door, he asked me what I was doing with the Polish luggage.

"It's a shopping bag," I said, knowing this homecoming wouldn't be any different from my others. "I had too many things to carry in my suitcase."

"It's Polish luggage," he said. "I used to see it all the time when I was flying, especially after the airline cut its fares and all the riffraff took to the skies."

Daddy said all this coolly, though his voice had deteriorated into a dry whisper because of his illness. He wore a dark blue stocking cap now that he had lost most of his hair. The suit that fit him so smartly when I was a child drooped around his shoulders.

"I just want the best for my little girl," he said. "Did Ross buy it for you? He always had expensive tastes."

I escaped to my old room, threw open the closet, flung the shopping bag inside, and started to close the door. My own face hung there like a death mask. I screamed. Mother burst into the room, saw me staring at the picture, and began sobbing in my arms. She explained that this was the remnant of a self-portrait I'd given her and Daddy when I was in school.

"You know that oval frame that Grandma gave me?" she said between sobs. "I thought your picture would look lovely in it."

"But Mother," I said. "That frame was a fourth the size of my painting."

"I know, but I thought if I trimmed it a little . . ." and she burst into tears. She hiccoughed the rest. She was almost hysterical. She pointed to my portrait and said in a weepy voice, "I couldn't throw it away because you painted it. And I couldn't put it in the frame because it looked too ugly. So I tacked it inside your closet door and thought you'd figure out what to do. But, oh, Allison, I made you look like the moon. Do you forgive me?"

"Poor Mother," I kept saying. Both of us were crying loudly by now. "Don't worry, I don't blame you," and I didn't. At that moment I was only glad that Daddy hadn't also turned me into an emotional shambles. The best way to survive in my family is to hit yourself over the head with a rock and wander around in an amnesiac daze. Still, I wish Daddy and I had gotten along better on that visit. At this point it's obviously too late for us to mend our differences.

The room grows silent and I see Mother looking

like Gloria Swanson in *Sunset Boulevard*, half-walking and half-sliding down the stairs while leaning against the bannister. She reaches the bottom and sets Daddy's urn on top of the dark wood post at the foot of the stairs.

"Thirty years ago today I fell in love," she announces weakly. She falters, and we stand around awkwardly while she stares at her feet. Then she looks directly my way and says, "It was a private day between Lester and myself, and nothing will bring that world back to me or Lester back to this world. But three months ago he passed on, and I've waited until today to let him go." Here she looks like she has a lot more to say, but she merely glances up at the ceiling and shakes her head. "I don't know. Maybe it wasn't such a good idea," is all she can manage.

"Your mother can get pretty dramatic, can't she?" says Ross as we're driving in the procession behind Mother, who's in a limo with the funeral director. Ross keeps his eyes on the road as he asks this and has almost no inflection in his voice. He knows this is the kind of question that can get him into trouble, but he's probably just anxious because neither of us has said a word since we left the house ten minutes ago.

When I don't respond, he rubs his beard as though someone's slapped it. "I'm not saying I'm unsympathetic," he says. "Please, don't misunderstand me, Allison. I'm all sympathy. All I'm saying is that she has a tendency to lay it on a bit thick."

"What can I say?" I tell him. "She's my mother. She's the kind of person who lays things on thickly. That's her nature."

"Now you're angry," he says, glancing at me.

"I'm not angry."

"All I'm saying is that I'm surprised that two people like your parents came up with a child like you."

I give him a look, and his face reddens through his beard.

"Look, all I'm saying," he says, his voice rising, "is that you're the total opposite of those two. You're completely unsentimental, and you've got sensible views. I just can't stand sentimentality. You want to know where sentimentality gets you? Have you ever heard that *Weltschmerz*-filled crap the Nazis yodeled to each other? The Nazis were the most sentimental people on earth. The person who finally destroys the world, you know what he's going to be doing? Whistling 'My Old Kentucky Home.' That's all I'm saying. I'm not saying anything against your parents, so you don't have to twist my words around."

"Shush, Ross," I tell him. "I haven't said anything."

"Well, why don't you?" he says.

"Okay, calm down," I tell him. My God, you'd think Ross was the one whose father had just died. I suppose I should be more upset, but maybe I'm still numb. They say that people feel numb when someone close dies. But Daddy and I haven't been close for several years, and if this is numb then it's not any different from the way I normally feel.

On the other hand, maybe I'm going a little nuts, so I unfold the map passed out to all the mourners, the map of Mother and Daddy's first date. Our route is marked in red, and there are small notations next to each point of interest. We're coming up on the first one, so I read aloud: " 'Sal's Steakhouse. Back when I met Lester, Sal's was the swankiest place in town. When Les brought me here, I was awfully impressed. Les ordered

74

the London broil and I had the trout. Sal himself, an old friend of Lester's family, came to our table and brought us a bottle of champagne. Then the band played "Two Sleepy People" at Lester's request. Les led me to the dance floor and I practically swooned in his arms. We could have danced all night.' "

Ross winces and says, "You see what I mean? I'm not doubting your mother's sincerity, but when I hear something like that I have a visceral reaction. I feel like I drank a vat of Kool-Aid or fell into a mountain of cotton balls or buttered the inside of my mouth."

"Now look who's being dramatic," I say. "Give her a break, Ross. You didn't have to come here today."

"You're angry."

"You're *making* me angry. Look, I don't disagree with you. Mother's definitely batty and she's making a fool out of herself with this first date business, but you only get to bury your husband once, so you're entitled to make a fool out of yourself. Who knows? When you die—"

"Hold your tongue," he says.

"Even so, maybe I'll decide to go in for the first-date motif, too."

"If you do," he says, "you won't be able to admit anyone under seventeen without parent or guardian, if you remember." He gives me a grin.

"You really think you're something, don't you, Ross?"

"Ah now, that's a loaded question," he says, taking one hand off the wheel and pointing to the roof. "I might think I'm a different something from the something you think I am. First you've got to define your something, and then I'll tell you whether or not I think I'm the same something. Which I probably don't, judging from your expression."

75

We drive past the Chinese restaurant that used to be Sal's. Now it's the Hunan Palace.

"Daddy hated the Chinese," I tell Ross. "When I was eighteen, we got into an argument about it. He told me I didn't know what I was talking about, that I'd think differently if I'd been in Korea. He actually ended up by calling me a Communist pinko. Can you imagine?"

As I'm telling Ross, I remember the argument, how frustrated Daddy and I were with each other. I kept telling him that he couldn't judge an entire people from a war experience, and he kept telling me that I couldn't judge his attitude unless I'd had a war experience. I told him I was lucky I hadn't been in a war, or else I would have come out warped like him.

Ross is talking to me, but I just look out the window at the passing buildings. How many of them were here when my parents were first married?

I remember Daddy telling me about Korea, how he was shot down, and how he made it back to American lines, but not before he strangled a Chinese soldier for his food. He never described exactly what happened, except to say that he sneaked up on the man. But now I see it clearly, the Chinese soldier resting on a rock, cleaning his rifle. His pack beside him. My father starving, stumbling out of the woods. A frozen lake. Snow on the rocky soil.

Why am I imagining this? The poor man. How horrible.

Ross is still talking, and I give him a reassuring smile. The great thing about Ross is that he never realizes when you're not listening to him. As long as he's sounding off and you're not disagreeing with him, he thinks you're a dazzling conversationalist.

"There's always a certain amount of parental baggage you're going to have to discard," he's telling me. "One time, Mom came home and made us start packing

76

because someone had told her that the revolution wouldn't begin until the middle class moved to the ghetto. Luckily we were able to talk her out of it. But on the whole, I'm happy with the way I was raised. Thanks to Mom and Dad, I don't have one iota of prejudice."

"That's absurd, Ross," I tell him. "Everyone has some prejudice."

"Not me," he says.

"What about when you walk down a city street at night and see someone who's different coming towards you. Black, Mexican, or Polynesian, for that matter. Doesn't that person scare you a bit more than someone who looks like you?"

"You're confusing the issue, Allison. I'm afraid of anyone walking towards me at night. I'm afraid when a cop walks towards me. That doesn't mean I hate cops, though I'm not terribly fond of them, I admit. But fear and prejudice are not the same."

"So if I jumped when I saw a Polynesian come out of the shadows while we were walking, you wouldn't think I was prejudiced?"

"I don't see what difference it makes," Ross says. "You're not at all prejudiced."

"What if I were?"

"A senseless question. You're not."

"But what if I were?"

"It would depend on how much. If a lot of your father had rubbed off on you then we probably never would have met. But that's not the case. You're perfect."

I shake the map out to study it. How dare he call me perfect. How can he expect me to be perfect, and why would he want a perfect person?

"Can you stand another sappy reminiscence from my mother?" I say after several minutes.

"Allison, all I'm saying—"

"I know, I know, all you're saying is that you're

embarrassed by sentiment, and you detest people who have imperfect views."

Ross glares, and I bend over my mother's map.

"The Parthenon," it reads. "Lester and I saw *Raintree County* here with Montgomery Clift and Elizabeth Taylor that night."

I pause and imagine Mother and Daddy passing popcorn down the row to Liz and Monty.

"It was a stunning film," I read on, "though Les and I weren't too intent on it. We were watching our own film called, *I Only Have Eyes for You.* Still, I've always been a big fan of Montgomery Clift, and I've rarely missed an opportunity to see him in a role. In later years, Lester and I were distressed that the Parthenon did not retain the grandeur of its glory days. Now it's a revival house that caters strictly to a homosexual clientele. Ah me!"

Oh, Mother. Ah me, indeed. I look up from the map and glance at the facade of the Parthenon, a place of brightly colored plaster and reliefs of young gods sprinting among Doric columnms. Monty Clift wouldn't be so out of place here as she thinks, but who'd have the heart to tell her.

At the airport the funeral director abandons Mother in the limo. He shuffles off to a metal building not much bigger than a public toilet and there has a gruff exchange with a young man standing by the door. Mother climbs out of the car alone, blinking in the late afternoon sun like someone who's just emerged from a cave after years of reclusiveness. She looks uncertain as I walk towards her, gives her disheveled hair a couple of quick pats, and averts her eyes. Before I can reach her, she sways, stumbles, and barely catches herself. That stupid mortician. I should report him to the funeral director's union, if there is such a thing. I run over to Mother and take her arm, but she looks at me uncomprehending. She holds the urn so it touches both of us. Her head lolls on my shoulder.

"Lester?" she whispers.

I look down at her and wonder if she knows I'm here, or if she thinks she's walking arm and arm with Daddy. I'm much smaller than he was, but still taller than Mother. Taller than most women I know. When I was fourteen I was nearly six feet. One day I came home crying and saying I was a freak. Daddy took me out on the patio, and we drank lemonade. For over two hours he fed me heroic tales of our Viking ancestors and tall warrior women.

"Your great-grandmother five hundred years back sailed around the world with Leif Erikson and drank the blood of short boys in their skulls. Do you think she worried how tall she was?"

I knew he was making it all up. Still, he made me feel that my height wasn't freakish, but something to be treasured, an inheritance he and I had in common.

"Need some help?" Ross says to me in a tone that's almost even, but off key just enough to show that I've hurt his feelings and he hasn't forgiven me yet. He'll exact an apology from me with one of his silences on the long drive home.

Ross takes Mother by the elbow and guides her towards the metal shed. But he barely touches her and looks straight ahead at the door like a furniture mover negotiating a piano through some particularly harrowing passageway.

Once inside, the three of us sit in metal chairs around a plain desk, behind which the funeral director sits folding his handkerchief into various shapes. He tells us in a detached voice what's going to happen to

Daddy. He keeps folding his handkerchief. First he folds it into quarters. He turns it over and folds it into eighths. He turns it over and again and folds it in half. He's molded his handkerchief into an impossibly tight shape. You'd think that something that small would lose all its contour, but he's made it into a perfect little rectangle. Slowly he unfolds the handkerchief and spreads it out across his desk, making sure there aren't any creases.

He stops the business with the handkerchief and I look up at his face. He's still talking, but I can't even hear what he's saying. I hate corrugated metal buildings. You'd think an airport could afford better material: steel or even concrete. Corrugated metal gets so hot in the summer and doesn't breathe and eventually just caves into a heap of rusted sheets. I thought only African countries had corrugated metal buildings, since the roofs make such a pleasant sound in a jungle downpour. Or so they say.

The little man behind the desk stops talking and sneers at me. A long way off a torrent pours down on thousands of corrugated roofs. The rain is relentless, but the children feel safe inside as long as their parents tell them stories and there aren't any leaks.

The man keeps on talking, though his voice is below the register of the rain. It's pointless to try to talk above it. But what about Daddy's plane? How will it fly? Maybe the man is telling us that. Try to listen. I cock an ear towards him like Daddy's setter, Asgaard, used to do when you said, "Outside?"

The man stops talking and sneers again so I sneer back. His expression changes, and he points to the door. I jump when I see the man at the door and reach out for Ross's hand. Ross looks sideways at me, his eyes narrow, and he just lets his hand lie motionless in mine.

Polish Luggage

"Of course, you won't be able to see the remains, so Lance will wag his wings," I hear from the direction of the desk.

I wonder why this man by the door has made an appearance. He doesn't seem to have any wings to wag. He's the only person in our group not dressed in mourning. He wears a light blue shirt and navy blue pants, and has a tie with a silver clip. The uniform's familiar. It's what Daddy used to wear on his flights.

Lance leers at me from the doorway and I leer back. Then he bends down through the small doorway and leaves us.

The shriveled man at his desk is folding his handkerchief again. Fascinating.

He's got it halfway to its little rectangle shape, but then he grabs it off the table as though the cloth has suddenly caught fire. He shakes it, brings it to his face, and lets loose with a jarring "kazoom!"

"Excuse me," he says in his tinny voice. He blows into his handkerchief, and stuffs it into his oversized suit.

"I have a year-round cold," he tells us. "It never goes away. That's because I have a deviated septum. I've got to get it operated on one of these days."

Ross, who's reddening through his beard, nods vigorously and says, "Well, yes, that's a good idea."

I look at Mother to see if she understands what they're talking about, but she's just staring out the window.

The funeral director gives an extended snort and sniffle without bothering to reach for his handkerchief. "This is all fine," he says. "All well and good. But there's no time to dilly-dally. It'll be dark soon and then where will we be? Won't be able to see a thing."

Where will we be. I imagine Ross and me in our car,

the long silence, the inevitable apology. I'm sorry I saw you differently from the way you wanted to be seen, Ross.

The funeral director approaches Mother and gently takes the urn from her. She hardly seems to notice and keeps looking out the window.

The man returns to his desk, opens a drawer, and takes out a folded shopping bag. He shakes this open with the same quick snap he used on his handkerchief. The bag responds with a loud crack. He sets the shopping bag on the floor, takes the lid off Daddy's urn, then sits down and starts to pour Daddy into the shopping bag.

Look how carefully he pours, like a man filling a thermos with coffee before leaving home for the day.

I feel like someone's just punched me in the back of the neck.

"Polish luggage!"

The funeral director jumps and almost drops the urn. Ross and Mother turn towards me.

The shriveled man looks shocked. He holds the shopping bag with Daddy in front of him like a shield.

"You little prune," I yell as I take three great strides towards him and rip the bag from his hands. "You can't take him up there in Polish luggage."

"Allison!" Ross yells. I've never seen him so horrified.

The funeral director bobs his head towards Ross and starts to make clucking noises. He takes out his handkerchief, blows into it, and keeps looking at me like an Arab through a veil.

Ross approaches me with his arms apart. What are his intentions? He wants to give me a hug. He wants to understand what I'm doing. I start swinging the shopping bag at him, and he backs off.

Polish Luggage

"Get back, Ross," I tell him.

He shrugs and sits down.

"Please, Allison," Mother says from her chair in a serene voice. "Behave. Give your father back to the man. It's almost dark."

What is she telling me to do? Give my father back to the man? What have I been doing? The shopping bag seems to drop of its own will onto the floor, spilling its contents everywhere.

"Now look what you've done," the little man at his desk tells me from behind his handkerchief.

Most of the mourners have gone home, and only a small clutch of us have gathered on this hill overlooking the municipal airport and the forest preserve. The Cessna glides above us. It makes two low passes before beginning its climb, then disappears while we shield our eyes against the sunset and search nervously.

"There it is," Ross says.

"Where?" I turn in the direction he's pointing, but I still can't see.

Mother's hand rests limply in mine.

"There," says Ross, pointing in another direction.

"Mother, you're not looking in the right place," I say, and she gives me the barest nod.

"He just wagged his wings," Ross says, touching my shoulder.

Mother doesn't seem to realize she's missed it. She stares intently at that same spot, and I'd never tell her to turn away now. I don't know what she thinks she's looking at, though I suppose we've both seen what we came here to see.

As I hold her hand, I try to imagine her with Daddy on this hill at sunrise thirty years ago today. What was she thinking of on that first date?

Did she imagine they'd raise a family? What kind of family did she want? It's not too hard to imagine. The Happy Child, a vague dash and scramble across the yard into Mommy's arms. Knowing Mother, this was how she would have seen it. But who did this child resemble? Most likely it was a faceless and genderless thing, conveniently buried in Mommy's arms so she wouldn't have to imagine too hard. Her picture was complete with Daddy smiling down on Wife and Child, calmly waiting his turn, his arms open wide enough to embrace the world.

Digging
A Hole

When Abby, my ex-wife, finally noticed me in her backyard, I was already two feet down. She opened the back door of her house and hurried out.

"Lawrence, what are you doing here?" she said, and positioned herself to my side, so I couldn't swing any more dirt from the hole.

"I thought I'd come over for a visit," I said. "I haven't seen you for a while."

"I know that," she said. "That's not what I'm talking about. What are you doing in my backyard?"

"Digging a hole," I said. I made a little sideways gesture with my hand and added, "You're sort of in my way."

Abby stood aside. "I can see you're digging a hole. Have you been drinking?"

"Yes, I've been drinking," I said. "But that doesn't enter into the matter. In fact, it's illogical. People don't go around digging holes just because they've had a few drinks. That's no reason to dig a hole. If it was, then the entire city would be covered with them."

"You're evading me, Lawrence," she said.

I could have argued with her on that point, but I didn't. The truth was I didn't know exactly why I was

85

digging this hole. I had inklings. I knew that I had been going mad for two and a half years, though the word *going* implies a steadiness of course, a graphlike climb towards some final and perfect state of mind. Actually, I had been going mad, off and on, for two and a half years, with long intervals of clarity and contentment.

I took a deep breath and surveyed the situation to see if my shovel had uncovered anything yet. Maybe I had dug up Abby, and she hadn't really come out of the back door of her house. This thought was childlike and illogical. I felt a bit like a child, doing what I pleased without thinking through the results. But Abby wasn't much of a playmate. Her look was stern and her posture was as stiff as someone in an old daguerreotype. She didn't at all match the clothes she was wearing: baggy suspender jeans and a red Missouri University T-shirt, with only the head of the school mascot sticking over the bib of her overalls as though he were hiding.

On the other side of Abby's Victorian-style house and the surrounding black iron fence, two children were passing by, both of them eyeing Abby and me intently. When I looked at them, Abby looked too, but quickly turned away. Then she made a nervous rubbing motion with her hands on her jeans as though she were wiping dirt away.

One of the children was a girl, and the other was a boy who seemed to be her brother. The girl was no more than five. She was barefoot and wore a shabby brown dress. She had long blonde hair and freckles, but she wasn't a cute little girl. Her expression was serious. Her nose was small and her ears were larger than they should have been. In one hand she carried a red plastic flag on a stick, and in the other a small grey slide viewer.

She seemed to be in charge of her brother, who was

three at most. He was naked, and he followed his sister silently and solemnly on a plastic scooter.

The girl stopped, waved her flag once, and shouted, "HO!" At this cue the naked boy stuck out his legs on the pavement and braked himself. The girl leaned against the fence and stared at Abby and me, while her brother waited stock-still on the sidewalk like a carriage horse with blinders on. He didn't seem interested in us any longer, but the girl watched us as though we were somehow exotic, like polar bears kept at a game park. She started waving her red flag at me, trying to keep my attention.

I turned away, resolved to block all distractions.

On the tip of my shovel was a fat earthworm. I shook it off onto the grass. Then I pointed to it.

"Do you know what happens when you cut a worm in two?" I said.

"Yes, I think so," said Abby.

I dug the tip of my shovel into the worm's midsection and split it in two. The two halves curled away from each other, and the separate ends swirled around like Roman candles.

"Does that worm look like it's having a good time?" I said.

"Lawrence," she said. "I think you should come inside. We can talk about whatever you like, even worms. I have some iced coffee, and Roy will be home soon."

I pointed to the two worm halves. Each was doing a little slither dance in jerky motions as though paying attention to some Calypso beat. "I'd like to meet the guy who said you could split a worm in half," I said. "See how he'd like it."

"This is all fascinating, I'm sure," said Abby. "Maybe we can talk about flies next."

"Yes, flies are very interesting," I said and started to dig again.

The girl at the fence shouted to me. "You digging to China?"

"My patience isn't boundless, Lawrence," said Abby, but she seemed to be referring to the girl, as though I were responsible for her.

"Do you know what happens when you put a fly in a glass of water?" I asked.

"I suppose it drowns," said Abby.

"Hey you," the girl shouted. "Can I help?"

"That's only the way it looks," I said. "When you submerge a fly in a glass of water, it's surrounded by a tiny air bubble which you can't see. So after a while, it looks as though the fly is dead, but not really. It's just fainted."

"Truly amazing," said Abby. "A fainting fly."

"I bet you don't know how to revive a fly," I said.

"If I knew, I'd be famous, I'm sure."

"No, it's really simple," I said. "You just cover the unconscious fly with a mound of salt. The salt dries up the water, and after about a minute, the fly comes up out of the salt, brushes itself off, and flies away."

"Hey you," the girl shouted.

"You're attracting attention, Lawrence," Abby said.

"She's just a kid. It doesn't matter."

"Can I come and help?" the girl said again.

"Sure, come on in," I said.

"No," said Abby. "Go on home. I'm sure your mother is worried about you."

The girl gave Abby a bewildered look. She waved her flag in the air and marched off. Her brother didn't follow her because he had fallen asleep at the wheel of his scooter.

"Hey, Jimmy," she said. "Wake up."

The boy lifted his head, saw his sister walking away, sat up straight in his seat, and pushed off after her.

After the two of them had left, Abby looked down at the hole. In a tone half-defiant and half-apologetic, she said, "This whole thing is incredibly masochistic. You're not going to be happy until you kill yourself."

I stopped for a moment, dropped the shovel, and grabbed her by the shoulders. I didn't handle her roughly, though she acted as if I were threatening her life.

"What? What is it?" she said.

"Abby," I said softly. "There are two reasons for a man to dig a hole."

"Lawrence," she said. "You've got to leave. You've just got to go now."

"Either you want to bury something," I said, "or you want to discover something. The action, the digging, is the same, but the results are entirely different."

I still held Abby by her shoulders, but she didn't seem tense and hard anymore. I felt as though her body were struggling to stay on the ground.

"This isn't healthy," she said. "Roy will be home soon."

I let her go and stepped away. "You want to know why I'm doing this?" I said.

"No, I don't think so."

"I had a dream."

"Please, not a dream," she said. "You know what I think of dreams."

"I dreamed that we were at a party, the three of us."

Abby started to turn away. I walked in front of her, not really blocking her, just getting face to face again. I still had the shovel in my hand. I propped it up against a small willow tree. The tree was old and stunted and had only two thick branches arching out from the trunk. Someone had built a small treehouse, now a bunch of rotting wooden planks, between the branches.

"Who built this treehouse?" I said.

"Some child, before we moved in," she said, not looking up.

"You should take it down," I said. "It's rotting. Some kid might get hurt on it."

"Yes, I suppose so," she said, but didn't seem to be paying attention to what she or I was saying.

Abby sat down on the grass by the tree. She started rubbing her feet. "My feet hurt for some reason," she said. "I don't know why. I haven't been standing too much." Then she added, "What were we doing at this party?"

"I don't know exactly," I said. "We were just surrounded by people, you, myself, and Andrew in the center of this circle. Andy held me by the leg and lifted me into the air. I felt amazed that he was there, and that he was doing this. And then he said. 'See how light you are.'"

"It was a good dream?" Abby said.

"It's the first dream I've had in a long time," I said. "I don't remember them anymore."

Abby stood and brushed off her legs. She grabbed my shovel. "This is cruel," she said. "This is my yard. This is Roy's yard. Go act crazy somewhere else." She turned away and walked back to the kitchen with the shovel in her hand.

I followed her inside, hoping to get the shovel away from her, but she carried it into the kitchen and wouldn't let go. So I talked calmly for a few minutes and promised I wouldn't upset her life. Then she settled down a bit. She gave me a beer and fixed a whiskey sour for herself. We both went into the living room and sat down opposite each other, me on the sofa, Abby in an easy chair. She propped the shovel like an imperial staff against the chair.

She tried to make light talk with me, but I couldn't keep my eyes off the shovel. She asked how my job was, and I told her I had been fired. She asked if I was seeing anyone, and I told her no one interested me. Then she asked if anything interested me, and I said, "Digging interests me. Digging interests me a lot. You should give me my shovel. I don't want to force it away from you."

"Can't you be sane for one moment?" she said. "Can't you at least pretend?"

"There," I said, smiling my hugest, most grotesque smile. "I'm sane as a bumblebee."

Just then Roy walked in. I'm sure the sight of me smiling hideously at his wife was a surprise, but he didn't show it. He seemed a bit dejected. He took off his jacket and threw it on the chair. "What a terrible day," he said, sitting down on his jacket. "The computer somehow erased chapter five of my book, or it's lost. I just can't seem to retrieve it."

"Oh, that's awful," said Abby.

"Yeah," said Roy. "And the worst part of it is that I put chapters four and six together, and the gap didn't seem to make any difference. Class went horribly too. We've been doing *Lear* for two weeks now, and this guy with the most vacant eyes in the world, a guy who hasn't said a word all semester, finally decides to speak up. He raises his hand, and I'm thinking, 'My God, this guy can't be raising his hand of his own free will. He must be under some voodoo spell or something.' But I call on him anyway, and he says, 'Mr. Frederickson, just when did Shakespeare write this stuff anyhow?' So I say, 'Well, he was an Elizabethan. He lived in the fifteen hundreds.' Now this guy's eyes get really big, and I'm thinking, 'Oh no, I've given him too much information. He's going to explode or something.' But then, do you know what he does? He says, 'He was a 'Bethan? You mean we've been talking about a *dead* man for half the semester?' " Roy jumped out of his chair. "What am I supposed to do with minds like that?"

Abby and I laughed. Roy started walking back and forth across the room, his shoulders hunched. He was biting his lip, his eyes were popped out, and his wavy blond hair was uncombed. From the few times I had seen him, I knew that this was his normal state.

He stopped in front of Abby and said, "What's Lawrence doing here?" He didn't wait for an answer. Instead he turned around and said, "You want to stay for dinner?" He said this tersely, cueing me that my answer should be no. I didn't blame him. After all, I was his wife's ex-husband, and I wasn't invited over much.

"Sorry, I've got plans," I said.

"Good, so do I," he said. "I've got to find chapter five. I know it's buried in there somewhere. Anyway, I hope the two of you had a nice chat while I was beating my brains against the wall all day."

"Actually," said Abby. "We haven't talked much."

"Yeah, I'm digging," I said.

Roy looked at me in a bored but tolerant way. "I'm digging too," he said. "Give me five, brother."

Roy turned to Abby again, and I could tell from the pause and the way his head moved that he was giving her some secret look or mouthing words. Then he noticed the shovel. "What's that for?" he said. "Has Lawrence been attacking you or something?"

Digging a Hole

"No," she said, grabbing the shovel handle and smiling reassuringly. "I just thought it looked nice here. Lawrence has been digging a hole in our backyard," she added.

Roy put his finger cross-wise under his nose and grunted. Then he walked slowly over to the couch where I sat. He took his hand away from his face and revealed that he was once again biting his lip. He sat down beside me, very close, and didn't say a word. Instead he just stared at me as though he were watching news footage of a war he was someday going to fight in.

Finally he spoke. "So, you're digging a hole, are you? I don't see anything too strange about that. What is it, some kind of bomb shelter?"

"No," said Abby. "He's not that crazy. He thinks it's some kind of therapy. It has something to do with Andrew."

Roy's eyes widened a bit. "I see," he said.

Abby swung the shovel against her hip and looked down at it, touching the shaft lightly with her fingers.

"Abby's never talked much about that," said Roy.

Abby leaned forward in her seat and some hair fell across her eyes. The moment was awkward for all of us.

When she lifted her head she didn't look at me. Instead she brushed her bangs away from her eyes and smiled at the ceiling. For a moment I thought I glimpsed one of the small scars which were usually covered up by hair.

"Well, you just have to adjust," she said. "For a while I thought it was impossible."

Roy looked across the room at her. "Yes," he said. "Abby's perfectly adjusted."

Abby looked at him in shock, as though he were giving away some great secret. I didn't understand what was going on between them. They seemed to be talking about something that didn't have anything to do with me, some long-standing argument.

"We're still young," she said. "The two of you are doing your best to make me feel old. I refuse to go crazy because of you, Lawrence."

I shrugged and said, "I just want to dig my hole, that's all."

Roy stood up from the couch and walked over to Abby's side. He bent down and kissed her like a father kissing his child goodnight. And then he took away the shovel and brought it back to me.

"When you're done," he said to me, "fill up the hole again."

Both Abby and I didn't know what to make of him. I had expected him to be suspicious, even angry with me, but he seemed completely sympathetic.

"What is this?" said Abby. "A conspiracy? You're both nuts. You can't just allow him to dig a hole in our backyard."

"What do you want me to do?" Roy said.

"Call the police. Get him out of here. At least you could hit him. I don't want him running around loose in my backyard."

"I don't think he's acting so sick," said Roy. "Maybe this will get it out of his system and he'll be all right afterwards." While he said this, he kept his eyes steadily on Abby. There was frustration in his voice, and there seemed to be more he wanted to tell her. Instead he turned to me. "We'll have to get together and talk sometime," he said. "Just the two of us."

Abby stood up from her chair, and for a moment she seemed to look around for the shovel as though she wanted to bash Roy over the head with it.

"You're a pig!" she shouted at him. "Can't you even act like a normal husband?"

"In your case," he replied calmly, "you don't know what normal is."

"Get out of here," she said to both of us.

Roy and I obeyed. He went off in search of chapter five and I went back to my digging. The digging went quickly, and as I bent my back and kicked my heel into the shovel, I felt I was really getting somewhere. The strangest thing about Andrew's death had always been that Abby never remembered that she was the one driving the car that night. She thought that I had been driving. While we were still married we hardly ever talked about the accident. She didn't even cry when she learned that Andrew had died, and later she made me think there was something wrong with me because I wouldn't let go of him.

A while later I looked up from my digging and saw the little girl with the red flag and slide viewer, her brother still tagging after her on his scooter. I guessed that they had gone home since I had last seen them, because the boy wasn't naked anymore. Now he was wearing jeans, a western shirt and a cowboy hat with a sparkling strap.

The girl looked at me from the sidewalk. Then she turned towards her brother and waved the red flag in his face, shouting, "HO!" Without hesitation she walked across the yard towards me, her manner very serious and assured as though she were a city official. When she was halfway across the yard, she turned around again, waved her flag, and yelled, "Giddyup!" to the boy, who was still sitting on the sidewalk. The boy headed across the yard, pedaling furiously but making very slow progress against the grass and the soft dirt.

The girl approached me and handed me her slide viewer. "Look," she said.

I put down my shovel and took the slide viewer out

of her hand. I tilted it up to the sky and saw a blotch of colors which, after my eyes focused, became the body of Charlie Brown. A white bubble protruded from his head, and he was saying something, but I wasn't sufficiently interested to find out his message.

I handed the viewer back to the girl and said, "Interesting," trying to inject some sincerity into my voice.

But the girl wasn't fooled. "That's Charlie Brown," she said.

By this time the boy had joined us. He looked suspiciously at me and then covetously at the slide viewer.

The girl took little notice of his arrival. Instead she put down her flag a moment and took a pack of gum out of a small pocket in her dress. While I started digging again, she unwrapped each piece of gum and popped it in her mouth. Her cheeks bulged and the little boy watched her with an expression of longing. He pulled at her arm, but she shrugged and said, "All gone."

The girl picked up her red flag again, walked up to me, and waved it in front of my groin. "HO!" she shouted.

"What does that mean?" I said.

"That means stop, stupid," she said, and then added, "Giddyup!"

"I should move?"

"Yes," she said with a look of disgust.

I put my shovel down and started to walk around the hole in a slow circle. Surprisingly, the boy followed me on his scooter, with that same solemn look on his face, as though we were participating in some military parade in Red Square.

When I returned to the girl, she said, "My name's Charlotte. Why are you digging?"

"Just to dig," I said.

Digging a Hole

"My parakeet died, you know," she said.

"Yes, I think I knew that," I said. "My little boy died. He was your brother's age."

"He was?" Charlotte looked over at her brother in a way that made his eyes bulge. He pedaled quickly away from her, then turned around and rode back in a straight line. For a moment I thought he was going to run her down, but he stopped just short of her. As an afterthought she said, "HO!" but without much enthusiasm. Then she took the well-chewed wad of gum and shoved it in her brother's mouth, saying, "Here!" in a tone of total disdain. The boy's eyes bulged again, but he didn't say anything. He started to chew.

"He never talks," said Charlotte. "He just watches and rides around and things like that. He's pathetic."

I laughed and said, "Where did you learn a word like that?"

"From my dad," she said.

Suddenly the boy got off his scooter and lunged for Charlotte's slide viewer, but she was too quick for him. She laughed and held it over her head, yelling, "HO! HI!"

The boy soon realized this tactic wasn't going to get him anywhere, and he sat down on his scooter again without making much of a fuss.

"He's pathetic," said Charlotte. "You can take him if you want."

The boy pedaled away from Charlotte and then back again. When he stopped I said, "What's your name?"

"His name's Jimmy," said Charlotte. "He never talks."

"How 'bout it, Jimmy?" I said. "Want to come live with me?"

Jimmy pedaled over to me. He looked back at his

sister and gave her a mildly defiant look. Then he stepped off his scooter and took my hand. He held me, at first uncertainly, by my thumb and forefinger, but then I maneuvered my hand around his and grasped it gently. His hand was pudgy and warm and wet with spittle. I hadn't felt anything like it for a long time, but I didn't let myself get too worked up. This was somebody else's boy, and he was only holding my hand because he wanted to make a stand against his sister.

"Jimmy," said Charlotte. "You come over here right now. He's pathetic, isn't he?"

"I don't think so," I said. "He happens to be the best scooter rider I've ever seen, and I've seen all the pros."

Jimmy nodded his head.

"I don't think he's ever going back to you, Charlotte," I said.

I looked down at Jimmy, hoping he wasn't going to start crying, but his face looked only a little bit resigned. He was the youngest fatalist I'd ever met.

Charlotte, on the other hand, looked alarmed. "You can't do that," she said. "Tell him I'll let him see Charlie Brown."

Jimmy made a move to join her, but I gently pulled him back and gave him a look. He didn't make another move, and stood his ground like a small Sumo wrestler.

"Jimmy," Charlotte pleaded. "Come here. Please. I'll let you see Charlie Brown."

Now I let Jimmy's hand drop. Delighted, he walked over to his sister. She turned away from him like the distraught heroine in a silent movie and handed him the viewer as though it were now contaminated. Then she turned towards me, her face red and furious, and I knew that she was going to start bawling at any moment.

"My parakeet died, you know!" she shouted.

I suddenly felt terrible for tricking her, for trying to control her emotions. Maybe I had just made things worse between her and Jimmy. Maybe she'd go home now and beat him up, out of humiliation.

"I'm sorry, Charlotte," I said. "Where did you bury him?"

She looked angrily up at me as though I'd asked the dumbest question in the world, and then she got a strange, thoughtful look in her eyes. She ran to the willow tree and shouted, "Here!"

I picked up my shovel and walked over to that spot. I started to dig and then I said, "Not here. Are you sure he's gone?"

"Sure I'm sure," she said and ran to a patch of grass. "Here," she said. "You better get him out because he's not dead yet."

I hurried over, but as soon as I got there, she went to another spot and said, "Not there. Here, dummy, here!"

"Oh no," I said. "I'm pathetic, aren't I?"

Charlotte laughed and said, "You sure are."

I felt a little tugging at my sleeve. I looked down and saw Jimmy pointing at his feet. "Here," he said softly.

Charlotte came over to us and I started digging again. For the next fifteen minutes the three of us ran around the yard, tearing up small patches of grass and pointing to new patches when we got tired of the old ones.

Finally, after doing sufficient damage to Roy and Abby's property, the three of us sat back on the grass and laughed. By that time, Jimmy was probably more excited than he'd ever been in his life. He was pointing in every direction, up at the clouds, to the telephone lines and the willow tree, and across the street, shouting, "Here, here, here."

The only place he didn't point was Roy and Abby's house, and I looked at it now. It was dusk, and the streetlamps had just turned on. One light was on in the living room. I stopped laughing and watched the light as though something unusual and mystifying were going on in there.

After a few more minutes, Charlotte and Jimmy stood up and started walking away. Jimmy headed solemnly to his scooter, and Charlotte grabbed her viewer and red flag off the ground. As they walked away, I waved to them and they waved back. Then Charlotte walked back towards me.

"Charlie Brown," she said, and handed me the viewer as though she were awarding me a medal for valor.

I took it and thanked her in the same serious manner. She looked at me for a moment and then smiled wryly as though she knew that she was only a child, and that children don't really know the importance of things, and that I'd be forgotten forever in a couple of days.

She walked back to her brother, who was waiting patiently for her on the sidewalk. She stood in front of him as though she were leading an army, and waved her flag in the air and shouted, "Giddyup!"

When they had disappeared, I walked over to the kitchen window and placed my shovel on the ground. Then I went around the house to the living room window. Abby was lying on the couch with one arm resting on her forehead. A spilled drink with ice cubes scattered about lay on the floor beside her. She had her legs straddled over one of the couch's armrests. Her legs were spread slightly, and she looked like an expectant mother who had been brought to the maternity ward and made to wait on the table even before the pains began. She was holding a toy, a plastic gun I recognized as one of Andy's, and she was turning it over and over in her hands.

Looking in on that scene, I knew what I had forced on her. I couldn't just go home again and leave her alone. So I took my Charlie Brown viewer and threw it in the deepest hole, and then I walked around to the front of Abby's house and knocked on the door, and waited there like a normal human being.

A Sentimental Wolf

The good people of Uncle Izzy's village didn't even know what was going on outside. A giant wolf, four stories tall, towered above their snow-covered huts. The wolf stood on stiff legs, teeth bared in a photo-booth grimace. Maybe it was cold, its teeth chattering, its legs nearly frozen. Other than the snarling beast, the scene looked peaceful. The villagers probably mistook the giant wolf's knocking knees for frozen branches snapping or the logs popping in their own fireplaces. Smoke rose from every chimney. That's probably what attracted the mutant wolf in the first place. A little warmth and human companionship.

Unfortunately, Izzy had not meant to create a science-fiction character, product of a nuclear accident, come to wreak havoc on his *shtetl*. The wolf was *supposed* to be looking down on the village from a hill far above it. So when Michael looked at this painting he tried to be generous. How difficult it must have been for the old man even to hold the brush, as he was arthritic, half-blind with glaucoma, and suffering from kidney disease. What an accomplishment for Izzy just to have completed it. That the wolf looked at all like a wolf was remarkable. That the town looked like a town was astounding. Especially for a man with no formal education. Michael was eternally grateful to his uncle, who had paid for *his* education after Michael's father died. And because of that gratitude, the painting hung in a place of honor in the living room, where it took up half the wall. Michael asked Sylvia, his wife, if she minded, but she said, "Of course not. He was your favorite uncle and so that's my favorite painting in the house."

"Not bad for an eighty-five-year-old man with arthritis, glaucoma, and kidney disease, is it?" he often said to visitors.

The only person who'd ever disagreed was Sylvia. One night she got woozy at a party and kept referring to Uncle Izzy's painting as "The Pogrom of the Mutant Wolf." She went on to say that the wolf looked like it was about to relieve itself on one of the huts. That remark wounded Michael. Although Sylvia claimed she adored the painting, Michael didn't believe her. What's more, he suspected she hadn't cared much for Uncle Izzy either. She'd only met him once anyway, after the stroke. He hadn't even recognized Michael on that visit and kept calling him Leonard, which was the name of Michael's father. At the time of their visit the wolf painting was relatively new and still hung in Izzy's house. As Michael admired it, the old man started shouting, "Put out the fire! Put it out!"

"What's wrong?" Sylvia said to Michael.

"The poor man," Michael said. "Light affects him strangely these days. He thinks the painting is on fire."

"Put it out!" the old man screamed.

"Do something, Michael," Sylvia said almost as loudly.

Michael drew the window shades and stood in front of the painting.

"See, Izzy?" he said. "It's only sunlight. I wouldn't let anything happen to your painting."

The old man calmed down, but Sylvia seemed spooked, and so Michael thought of an excuse to leave. Not that it mattered. The old man hardly seemed aware of anyone's presence anymore.

"Look at him," Sylvia whispered as they were leaving.

Michael knew what she meant. The old man still wasn't convinced that his painting was safe. But now he sat quietly on the couch, hands trembling on his knees, as though resigned to the fact that the village in his painting was being devoured by flames.

After Izzy died, Michael claimed for himself the most awkward of Izzy's worldly goods. Why Michael felt so connected to the painting he couldn't say for sure, though he was certain that Izzy's presence lived on somehow in its clumsy brush strokes.

Izzy was the person who taught Michael that objects have souls. He used to talk of his early days in America, as a young man in Bensonhurst. At that time, Izzy and his brother Chaim once saved their money and bought a canoe. They used to paddle out to Staten Island for picnics. One day the canoe was stolen. They found it the next week on the beach, battered, dented, and pocked with holes. No one ever found out who had murdered it, but Izzy and Chaim buried their canoe in the backyard by the chicken coop, with a full ceremony attended by everyone in the family.

Besides containing Izzy's soul, the painting gave Michael a sense of loss for the world it portrayed. He had never known the name of Izzy's town, but he liked to imagine its inhabitants hanging upside-down, Chagall-like, in the sky, or wrestling with *dybbuks* in the snow as in some Singer story. The four-story wolf he took as a symbol for the Cossacks ready to storm the village at any moment.

104

There were times when these notions seemed laughable, even to Michael. Sometimes he admitted to himself that the wolf was just a wolf, not a symbol for anything, but the accident of an amateur artist with a poor sense of perspective.

Other than Uncle Izzy's wolf painting, you couldn't fault the decor in Michael and Sylvia's home, which was adobe colored outside with windows the size and shape you'd find in the turret of a castle. Inside, ceiling fans brushed the air across uncluttered floors made of blue Mexican tiles. Sylvia kept the house dry and airy, like a desert with its neat pockets of life: a yucca plant by the living room couch, a miniature orange tree in the family room. The entire house seemed self-satisfied, with the aura of a successful dieter. It was the kind of house that made you feel svelte when you entered. Michael and Sylvia felt very svelte when they walked around on the cool tiles in the clothes they ordered from Banana Republic. Michael spent much of his time in Outback Pants and Naturalist Shirts, Foreign Legion Shoes and Safari Caps. Sylvia often did light housework barefoot in Fatigue Pants and an Expedition Shirt. When she went shopping, she brought her Low-Profile bag with her. Other than Izzy's wolf, which was sacred, there wasn't one thing in the house that was corpulent or high-profile.

But the svelteness of the house was threatened the day Great-Aunt Elke died, leaving Sylvia her most prized possession. Michael might have been able to convince Sylvia to ditch the treasure if it had been left by any other relative. This belonged to the legendary Tante Elke, his wife's favorite aunt, whom he'd only met twice, once at their wedding ten years earlier and again at the funeral of Elke's husband, Simon, two years ago. For weeks after Elke's death, Michael was barraged by a cavalcade of Tante Elke stories. Not that he was unsympathetic. He was all sympathy, but Sylvia, in her grief, forgot how many times she'd told Michael the same Aunt Elke stories. Some of them he heard once a day for two weeks, which made him feel like he was going through some kind of ideological indoctrination.

Still, he had favorites, like the tale of Aunt Elke's arrest by the Nazis and her separation from her son at Bergen Belsen. By all rights, her son should have died right away. He was only thirteen, and the Nazis killed children immediately. But he looked sixteen, and he was strong, so they made him a slave laborer. Both he and Elke survived the Holocaust, but neither of them knew the other was alive. Fifteen years later in Tel Aviv, they ran into each other, completely by coincidence, on a busy street.

Then there were subtler, less remarkable stories about Sylvia as a little girl, when she spent summers at Elke's house on Long Island. Michael heard a full inventory of the house, from Aunt Elke's deluxe organ with its built-in tape recorder to a music-box teapot that played "Tea for Two" when you lifted it, and a liquor cabinet that had a hand-painted scene on it. The painting showed an eighteenth-century couple dancing a minuet in the midst of a shadowy clearing. Each dancer held a hand high in the air, the woman lightly touching the man's. The woman stared at her partner, but he looked away towards the woods. When the cabinet door opened, the dancers parted, the woman still holding the man's fingers. As a girl, Sylvia had assumed that the woman in the painting was Aunt Elke, and that the man was her first husband, Abe, who had been killed in the Holocaust. Why she thought the man was Abe, she didn't know. Only he didn't look like her second husband, Simon.

Through a constant pummeling of sentimental details about Aunt Elke, Michael started feeling an odd admiration for the old woman. He listened patiently to Sylvia's stories, and each time he heard one over, he acted like it was the first time. Often he found himself nodding like a child being told a familiar bedtime story. "And then what happened?" he'd say.

One night Sylvia said, "What do you mean what happened? I was asking if you minded. I found out today."

The two of them were in the living room watching a Miss Marple episode on "Mystery!" This was part three of a three-part series. Unfortunately, Michael hadn't seen the first two, though Sylvia had seen the whole series before. She had been chatting in a low-key way during the whole program, while Michael had been trying to figure out who was who and what had happened rather than who done it. Who done it was beyond him. So far, all he could figure out was that someone people called "The Dumb Swede" or "The Idiot Norde" or "The Bumbling Finn" (the name had only been given once) had been murdered at a party when the lights went out. Someone at the party had murdered him. Now, a young couple was being confronted in a drawing room by a rich-looking elderly woman with a string of pearls around her neck. Apparently, the two weren't who they claimed they were.

"We were planning to tell you right away," said the young man, "but then came the murder, and we thought they'd naturally suspect us if they found out we'd been lying about our identities."

"Why did you lie then?" the old woman said stonily.

"You see, we're in love," the young man said.

"I see," the woman replied.

Sylvia sat beside Michael on the couch. She was barefoot and had her feet tucked under Michael's rump. "I know an organ wouldn't exactly fit in here," she was saying.

Michael clasped his hands over the back of his neck and leaned forward.

Sylvia's words intruded, and he imagined a slab of someone's liver displayed on a dish on the coffee table.

"You're right. It wouldn't fit," he said.

Now another man entered the room and said, "Murgatroyd's been murdered."

The old woman reacted with a look of horror and put her hand to her neck. "Oh no, not Murgie. That's horrible." She twisted her pearls so violently that they snapped and fell on the floor. "I'm so frightened," she said, her hand still clasped to her neck, and ran from the room.

"Who *is* this woman anyway?" Michael added, trying to remember if he'd seen her before.

"Tante Elke," Sylvia answered.'

Michael figured the pearls must be a clue.

"It's *her* organ," Sylvia said.

Why had she kept her hand around her neck? What was her name? "I didn't know she had a donor card," he told Sylvia finally.

"What are you babbling about, Michael?" Sylvia replied. "I was referring to the organ in Tante Elke's house. The one I told you about. It's my legacy."

Sylvia picked up the remote control, pointed it at the TV, her arm straight, and assassinated the picture.

"I was watching that," Michael said.

A Sentimental Wolf

"It was the old woman," replied Sylvia. "She wasn't who *she* said she was either. Actually, she was pretending to be her dead sister, because her sister had inherited a lot of money from her husband. She killed those other people to protect her false legacy. That's all people kill each other for. Legacies and love. There. Now you know more than anyone."

Sylvia reached for a magazine on the coffee table and started flipping through it.

"Oh, I wasn't interested in the show anyway," Michael said, leaning back on the couch.

She put down her magazine, smiled, and repositioned herself on the couch so that she faced Michael. "Good," she said. "Now we can talk about *my* legacy. It's Tante Elke's organ."

"We'll find room for it," Michael said, trying to imagine where an organ would possibly fit.

"You really think so?" she said.

"I just said so."

"But I want you to be sure. Think about it. I want you to picture what an organ would look like in here before you say yes."

Three organish pictures came to mind: a pipe organ in a cathedral, a demo of "There's No Business Like Show Business" at a music store in the mall, and Lon Chaney as the Phantom of the Opera going "Ha cha cha cha cha!" like Jimmy Durante as he spun on his organ stool, his ghoulish fingers prancing.

"We'll find room for it somewhere," Michael said.

"What do you mean somewhere?" Sylvia said, leaning towards him.

"Okay, anywhere. I just meant that we'll have to find room for it."

"What if you think it's ugly?" Sylvia said.

"What do you want, a blood oath that I'll love it?"

Sylvia nodded and picked at a fingernail.

"What about her teapot that plays "Tea for Two" when you lift it?" Michael said. "Are we inheriting that, too?"

"That's for my mother," she said. "And my brother gets the hand-painted liquor cabinet. The organ is mine."

"But you don't even know how to read music," Michael said. He knew he was into dangerous territory.

Sylvia picked up the magazine again and started turning its pages. Michael glanced over and saw a blur of photos of young women with glad expressions, their arms wide, their clothes billowing. Sylvia stopped at a photo of a woman striding along in leopard-spot stockings and the words between her legs: "High-Profile Pattern Mixes." Sylvia seemed to study the photo intensely for a moment, as though the glad-faced jungle woman were a daughter from whom she'd been separated years ago. Abruptly she put the magazine on the coffee table, and said, "Once we've got the organ, I'm sure I'll learn how to play it."

Sylvia came into the room with drinks for the two movers, a balding man in a blue jumpsuit that was covered with sweat spots, and his teenage partner. The older man gulped his drink down in seconds, handed back his empty glass to Sylvia, and said with a slight Irish accent, "That was delightful."

The teenager tilted an ice cube into his mouth and sucked on it while placidly studying Uncle Izzy's painting. Then he set his empty glass down on top of the organ.

Sylvia swept up the boy's glass and said, "I'll get you both refills."

"No ice this time, please, ma'am," the older man called after her.

Michael didn't understand why Sylvia was so worried about the kid setting down his drink on the organ. It was squat and fat, made out of a dull wood marred by innumerable water marks. A very high-profile item, the organ had a vaguely human quality. Actually, it looked like some kind of gremlin. In some ways it reminded Michael of Aunt Elke herself. Just as married couples grow to look alike and pet lovers become like their dogs and cats, the same must be true of people and their instruments. He imagined Aunt Elke, as squat as her organ, seated at the bench, a cup of hot water and lemon sloshing out of the cup as her overripe legs vigorously pumped the organ's pedals.

Michael approached the boy and pointed to Izzy's painting. "Not bad for an eighty-five-year-old man with glaucoma, arthritis, and kidney disease, is it?"

The boy shifted his ice cube to his cheek and shook his head.

"Not bad, indeed," said the older man with an appreciative smile. "Is the artist a relative of yours?"

"Was," said Michael. "My great-uncle Izzy. Not only did he have glaucoma, arthritis, and kidney disease, but the old boy was recovering from a stroke when he finished that one. It was the last painting he ever completed."

Actually, it was also the first painting he ever completed, and the stroke had come after he'd finished the painting, not before. But Michael only wanted people to be as impressed by the painting as he was. For Uncle Izzy's sake.

The older mover shook his head. "Some of history's greatest accomplishments have transcended the depths of human infirmity and despair," he said.

The boy gave his ice cube a loud suck and tucked it back in his cheek. "No kidding," he said. "He had all that arthritis and stuff when he painted it?"

"Not only that," said Sylvia, returning from the kitchen with the drinks, "but also diphtheria, meningitis, and whooping cough."

Michael couldn't believe she had said that. Some things you don't make fun of: handicaps, sexual perversions, and Uncle Izzy's painting, among them. Sylvia hadn't spoken that way since her crack about the "Pogrom of the Mutant Wolf." And he'd only forgiven her for that because she'd been drunk. Maybe she was drunk now in a different way. Maybe she was drunk at having Aunt Elke's ugly organ here. Still that was no excuse.

Sylvia looked over at Michael, smiled and winked. He looked away to let her know what he thought of her joke.

"That's decent," said the boy. "I really like that wolf."

"Don't set your drink down on the organ," Sylvia cautioned.

"Yeah, okay," he said and set it down anyway. "But you know what that wolf looks like?"

"It's time for us to be on our way, Ronnie," the older man said. He handed Michael a pen and a clipboard. "If you'll just sign right here. It states that we delivered the instrument and you found it to be in good condition."

Michael took the pen and signed the bill, though he was bothered by the boy's comment, and wanted to know what he meant.

"It's a lovely instrument, ma'am," the older man

112

said to Sylvia. He took back his pen from Michael and stuck it in the pocket of his jumpsuit. "They don't build them like that anymore. Do you happen to know if it was made in the States or Europe? It has a bit of a French flavor to it, wouldn't you say?"

"It was made in Hoboken, I think," said Michael. "That must be the flavor you're alluding to."

Michael looked at Sylvia and smiled.

"Hoboken," said the man and laughed.

After the movers left, Sylvia turned to Michael. "What was that Hoboken remark about?"

"What was that crack about diphtheria and whooping cough?"

"I don't know what you're talking about. You've probably never even been to Hoboken."

"I was in Hoboken once," Michael said.

"Yeah, and that makes you an expert," said Sylvia.

Sylvia plugged the organ into an outlet and sat down on the bench. For a while, neither spoke. Only once had he seen an object that disturbed him more: his grandmother's armadillo basket. It had been made from an armadillo by hollowing out the stomach and curving its tail into its mouth for a handle. The legs had been cut off and glued onto its back to make it stand. The color of stone-ground mustard, it shed shellac when you touched it. The basket even had hairs sticking out between the armor plates. His grandmother stored letters in it. She loved it because it reminded her of Cuba. Michael's mother told him that "some Cuban gigolo your grandmother met in Havana gave it to her after a night on the town." A strange present to commemorate a special evening, Michael thought, but he couldn't argue with her. When his grandmother died, the armadillo basket was thrown out, and now, fifteen years later, Michael wished he could see it again. He felt as though his grandmother's soul had been thrown on the trash heap along with the basket.

He wondered what household object his spirit would live on in after he died. That was something you couldn't predict, but he hoped it would be the humidor that Sylvia had given him for their seventh wedding anniversary.

A hellish sound suddenly came from the organ, a high-pitched voice accompanied by the watery strains of an out-of-tune keyboard. The percussion behind the organ was out of synch with the music.

"Is that you?" he said to Sylvia.

The volume went down by half and Sylvia turned around on the bench. "I pushed a button," she said, "and the tape deck started."

Michael concentrated. It sounded like fusion jazz. It sounded like something—in an awful lot of pain. A mule that had run a long way up a hill and collapsed. The mule was stretched on its side, its thin legs distended, breathing in and out in gasps, its purplish tongue hanging from its mouth.

"It sounds like . . . yes it is. . . . It's 'Heart and Soul' ", said Sylvia.

Michael tried to hear "Heart and Soul" but all he could make out was the mule going, "WHEE-haw, haw, Whee HAW haw haw haw haw, WHEE-haw haw, Whee-HAW haw haw haw haw, WHEE-HAW, WHEE-haw Whee Haw, Whee haw, WEE . . . wee wee . . . wee wee . . . wee wee wee wee." A snare drum set stood next to the mule, some drummer keeping time as the animal wheezed. Behind the dying mule and the drum set, a woman hummed.

Michael joined Sylvia at the organ and said, "Could we turn it down a hair? Just so the tone comes in better?"

"I can barely hear it now," said Sylvia.

Michael looked over the machine. The sound came from a speaker set into the organ. Next to the speaker was the tape deck itself, built into a little cubby on the right of the machine. A row of percussion knobs occupied a cubby on the left side. In the middle were two rows of keys.

"That's Tante Elke," Sylvia said, looking up at him. "That's her voice in the background."

The drink Sylvia had given the teenage mover still sat on top of the organ. Michael grabbed the drink and sniffed as though he were a royal food taster. He just wanted something to wet his mouth, but there was no telling what kind of germs the kid had. So he just held it in his hand while he listened.

After a minute the song ended. Someone called the SPCA. The mule was put to sleep.

Another mule rose up on uncertain legs and brayed a mourning song for its dead comrade. This time Michael could make out—"The Sound of Music"—because Aunt Elke blasted it out as though she was trying to bring down an Austrian mountain with her voice. Michael imagined her singing with her arms wide as she jounced up her mountain trail on the back of a loaded-down mule. Actually her singing wasn't half as horrible as her organ playing. Maybe Elke had always been a lousy keyboard player, but had at one time a good singing voice. She'd obviously had some training. Her tone was strong and resonant, though only half the notes she hit were true ones.

Michael brought the mover's leftover soda to his lips. He paused before he took a drink. It couldn't hurt, he thought, taking a tiny sip. He just needed something to wet his lips.

Abruptly the clamor from the tape stopped. No

more dying mules. No more Aunt Elke, though white noise still cascaded from the speaker.

"Is it done yet?" Michael said.

"It's still turning," said Sylvia. "I hope it's not broken."

Michael's mouth moistened slightly at the thought.

"There's someone at the door!"

The words startled Michael, and Sylvia jumped slightly on the organ bench.

"What?" he said and started heading for the front door.

Michael realized the voice didn't belong to Sylvia. She looked up at him. "That's her," she told him.

"I said, there's someone at the door," the voice yelled again. "Are you deaf?"

"All right, give me a moment to get there," said a man's voice from a distance.

"My God, that's my Uncle Simon," Sylvia said. She reached up and clutched Michael's hand. "She must have forgotten she had the practice tape in the machine. I hope she doesn't remember to turn it off," she added.

"I thought he was dead," Michael said, taking another sip of his drink.

Sylvia let go of his hand and waved at him like he was a gnat. "Sssh," she said. "They're both dead."

"That's not what I meant," Michael said. "He died before she did. What's this tape doing in the machine?"

"Hush!" Sylvia said.

Uncle Simon said something garbled.

Sylvia looked up at Michael. "Did you hear what that was?"

"Beats me," he replied. "It sounded like 'Look sharp, me buckos.'"

"Maybe it was Yiddish," said Sylvia.

116

For a moment there was silence, and then Uncle Simon's voice boomed, "I'm not going deaf."

"I always have to yell to get your attention," said Aunt Elke. "If that's not deafness then what is it?"

"Insanity. It says here in the paper that the Japanese kill each other all the time over piano noise."

"This is an organ," she said. "It's supposed to be soothing."

"Learn something different at least," said Simon, his voice tense and hoarse. "Oh, it's no use arguing with you."

"Go answer the door," said Aunt Elke. "Don't have a conniption."

Only Aunt Elke's raspy breathing could be heard for the next minute. Michael imagined her sitting at the organ with a grimace, waiting for her husband to return from the door.

"HA!" Uncle Simon's voice boomed from the speaker. "That was Mrs. Hoy. She says that you're giving Blackie nightmares."

"When did Blackie start telling Mrs. Hoy his nightmares?"

"Ask Mrs. Hoy. Just stop your racket. The whole apartment building agrees. Even the dogs."

"You're making it up."

"See for yourself. That was Mrs. Hoy I was speaking with."

"It was probably Blackie."

"Dogs don't ring doorbells," said Simon. "People do."

"It's a smart dog," Elke replied.

Sylvia punched the stop button on the tape player.

"It's not over yet," said Michael. "Let's hear some more."

"The quality isn't good," Sylvia said. "We'll play it some other time."

"The quality's fine. Don't you want to find out what happened?"

"I don't feel we should," said Sylvia. "I never heard them say a harsh word. They were devoted."

"I'm sure they were," said Michael. "But everyone argues."

"I guess you're right," she said. "I suppose it can't hurt anything," and she pushed the play button.

"You give dogs nightmares. You give me nightmares," Uncle Simon said.

"I have nightmares, too," said Aunt Elke. "I have them every night." Her voice was softer now. "I play because it soothes me. It's the only thing that does."

"It was a mistake," said Uncle Simon. "I never should have bought it for you. It'll kill me before the year is out."

"So wear your earplugs. Go for a walk."

"I'll go for a walk."

"Good."

"You want to know what the real mistake was?" Elke shouted.

"What? Tell me."

"No, get out of here."

"Tell me."

"Go on."

"I want to hear you say it."

"Say what?"

"The mistake! The mistake!" Simon shouted.

Michael dropped the glass he was holding. It shattered on the keyboard and liquid flew everywhere.

Sylvia jumped.

Michael looked down at the keyboard and saw a

spreading hand of liquid seeping into the built-in tape recorder.

Sylvia popped out the cassette and turned it over. "You've ruined it. It's soaked."

"It was an accident."

"An accident. I've never had an accident with your four-story wolf, and that's been in the house five years. This organ was here an hour, and now you've ruined it."

"I'll clean it off," Michael said.

"But the tape," said Sylvia, crying. "That was my aunt's voice. I'll never hear it again." She ran upstairs and slammed the bedroom door.

Michael went to the kitchen for a dish rag. He ran some water on it and returned to the living room. He wiped off the organ, and then he cleaned some liquid that had dripped onto the Mexican tiles.

After he had finished, Michael sat on the couch, staring at Aunt Elke's organ. He wondered how he'd ever get used to its heavy presence in his airy house. Sentimental treasures were supposed to bring people together. He should have said no in the beginning. The whole thing had been a mistake. Now Sylvia would probably want to learn how to play the thing just to spite him. She was like that sometimes.

Why was he thinking like some bitter old man? Maybe he'd go for a walk to clear his head.

"Go ahead. Go for a walk," he thought even more bitterly. "Drown in the lake. Get run over by a bus."

Intuitively he looked towards Uncle Izzy's painting. Izzy wasn't there. Just some dumb animal that couldn't speak its mind.

The Trumpet
Player and
His Wife

I heard them almost every
night, crashing through my ceiling like some novel of
the Roaring Twenties too thick and ambitious to hold its
bindings. It sounded as though they were moving furniture, loads and cartons of books and beds and ele-
phant geraniums. I didn't know what they were doing
up there. They looked like such a gentle couple, he with
his happy carnival face and his well-kept appearance,
and she with her manicured nails and some kind of
cleaning utensil always in her hand. If they were making love up there, then I had them completely wrong.
Maybe they were unhappy with their lives. Perhaps
they had lost sense of themselves somewhere along the
way. Or maybe they were making love *and* moving furniture, trying to settle into something else, moving each
other around, trying to make it stick this time. And
thinking this, I moved carefully around my apartment,
imagining each movement as a decoration of sorts, each
footstep a new approach. After it was over and all the
furniture had been moved upstairs, I heard different

sounds. The man played his trumpet, not intricate jazz riffs, but always the same thing, a simple scale repeated again and again like a furniture mover returning up the same flight of stairs to see if he had left anything behind.

What's That in Your Ear?

❦

On the Brewer side of my family, I'm related to two famous people: Houdini and, according to legend, Attila the Hun. From these two strains have emerged a fine blend, personified in the lives and characters of my great-uncles Tony and Maury and my great-aunt Rose. It's like a nice coffee mixture: a little bit of Houdini, a pinch of Attila, and a bunch of beans of undetermined variety. With Houdini, you've got the flamboyant magician always trying to prove that he can escape from his own prisons. Then there's Attila going around destroying or conquering the more civilized nations. And to what purpose? So that he can set up his own mediocre dynasty of barbarians who eventually get co-opted and wind up spending winters at the Ma-Ho-Pa Spa in Desert Hot Springs. Collapse history for a moment and take a snapshot of Maury, Tony, and Rose standing next to their kinsman, Atilla, the Scourge of God. And down in the corner, who's that struggling with a set of handcuffs and chains underneath those curative mineral waters?

It's me. I come up out of the water and dry myself off. I've just seen another family member, my cousin

Lenny, walk past me towards the sauna. I call out to him, but he doesn't hear me. I've been trying to corner him all day without the others around. I haven't the faintest idea why he's come all this way to visit, especially since he's not well-liked, but I'm glad he's around. He's the only normal person here besides me.

Lenny is my first cousin, once removed, dismembered, and replaced. I've only seen him half a dozen times in my life, and he's known as something of a character in my family. Even a family of characters has its own characters. The big thing that everyone disapproves of is that he's a musician. Last time I saw him was at my grandmother's house in Long Beach, Long Island, when I was eleven. He tried then to interest me in learning the guitar, but I was temporarily obsessed with a printing press Maury had bought for me. Lenny showed up that time with his wife, Allison, who talked incessantly to my bewildered grandmother about G-spots. I reported it all, including the G-spots, in the first and only edition of my hand-set newspaper, *The Daily Son*.

Now he's here and things are different. He and Allison split up a year ago. She went to Israel and joined a group of Lubovitchers. Supposedly she's already remarried and wears scarves all the time. As for me, I've been sent to live with my uncles and aunt until my parents can deal with me again. They've made a mistake, exiling me like this. If I ever return, I plan to be twice as bad. Then where will they send me? Next time they'll have to give me a lethal injection. But for now, I'm a prisoner being brainwashed into thinking I'm seventy years old. For the last few months I've been playing shuffleboard and a Hungarian card game called Kalooki and eating special food for the elderly that's delivered every night to the spa: a lot of creamed corn and chipped beef. Things that are easy to chew.

On my way down the steps to the saunas, I pass Aunt Rose in her one-piece bathing suit sitting on a small bench on one of the landings. She's looking out toward the mountains. When she sees me she smiles and says, "I could sit and watch these mountains forever."

"You'd rot before long," I tell her.

She just shakes her head and says, "Such a mouth," and I run on down the steps. To me, the only interesting thing out here are the roads. The roads back East fit into the landscape, but in the desert you can see them for miles until they reach the mountains and stop dead in front of them. They look like little cut-out strips of paper some kid has pasted onto a piece of cardboard. I like to imagine them blowing off or catching fire and turning into ashes and swirling into the sky.

I open the door of the sauna and step inside. A bunch of steam pours out and around me, and the hot cedar-shaved air goes down my throat like one of those force-feeding tubes.

"Lenny," I call, and start opening doors to the individual sauna rooms. There's absolutely no one around. The benches are empty. It's just the steam and heat and me. No Lenny, even though I saw him come down this way. I'm alone for the first time in days, and suddenly I get this incredible craving for a cigarette. What a weird place this would be for a smoke. It would just blow out your lungs, like sucking on an M-80.

Since I don't have any cigarettes in my bathing trunks, I go back outside and head for the swimming pool. Rose is sitting there now, and she tells me she saw Lenny head for Maury and Tony's room.

I enter their room without knocking, and when the

three of them see me, they stop talking. Lenny's in a chair by the TV, and Maury and Tony are facing him, sitting on their beds. Tony's got a drink in his hands, though it's only early afternoon. The two brothers have solemn looks on their faces, which isn't anything out of the ordinary. Tony has a face like a walnut: brown, round, and ridged. Maury looks more like a filbert. He's mostly bald, and his face is smooth and long.

"I was just looking for you," I tell Lenny. "I thought you'd gone in the sauna."

Lenny sighs and stands up instead of answering. Then he runs his hand through his long blond hair and afterwards rubs his fingers together as though they've picked up some grease.

"I don't think there's anything more to discuss," Maury tells Lenny.

Lenny looks at the ceiling and then down at the floor. "I guess I'll have to think about it," he says.

"Think," says Tony harshly.

"I think I'll take a swim," says Lenny. As he's leaving, he smiles at me.

"I think I'll take a swim too," I say.

"You were just in the pool." says Maury. "You'll get waterlogged."

"He's been in there all day," says Tony. "He's become a regular water rat."

Before I have a chance to follow Lenny out the door and escape, Maury fires off his next question.

"What kind of bathing trunks are those? You can see everything."

"What's there to see?" says Tony.

I look down at my bathing suit. I have no idea what they're talking about. But I go into the bathroom and change.

125

When I come out, Tony sets down his drink and pretends to choke.

"What's that you're wearing now?" says Maury, taking his brother's cue. "It looks like something a queer would wear."

My clothes aren't so strange. I've got on a pair of jeans, a T-shirt, and the brass earring I picked up at a street fair a couple of years back.

"It's no big deal," I say. "Everyone's wearing stuff like this."

"Everyone," says Tony in a high, effeminate voice.

"I'm not wearing it," says Maury. "I wouldn't be caught dead wearing an earring in my ear."

"How about your nose or your cucumber?" I say.

"Not to mention your hair," he continues, "which made you look like a half-shorn sheep when you got here. At least it's grown out some."

Now the battle has begun in earnest. I'm sure he heard my insult, but he's pretending I didn't say a word. I've gotten to Tony though. He looks a little confused and dazed.

"Okay, I'm a queer then. Whatever you want. Get me a drink, Tony."

For a moment Tony starts to obey me, but then catches himself and pours himself another shot instead. He lifts it in the air to me and says, "You're too young to drink. What would you want with a drink anyway?" Suddenly he grimaces, says, "ooch" with a great intake of breath, and bends over his stomach to massage his leg. Maury pretends not to notice.

"Someday, someone's going to start believing your stupid remarks," Maury tells me. "You want to wind up like your cousin Lenny, shooting dope and singing in a band?"

"I've done a lot worse than that," I say.

126

"Mr. Big," says Tony. Then he goes "ooch" again and starts rubbing his leg violently. "This darn leg. Ought to have it looked at."

"Heroin's really not as addictive as everyone says," I tell them. "Those horse trancs are what you've got to stay clear of. They make you nuts. I tried to shove a lightbulb down my friend Billy's throat. I don't even know where the lightbulb came from. The next night we tried ludes, and that's when I had my gay experience, but that was the only time. Mostly, Billy and I get our kicks from this hooker named Wanda. She doesn't have any teeth. You want to know why?"

"Where did you learn to talk like that?" says Tony, shaking his head. Then he looks at Maury and says, "I guess it's time for the Cloak of Invisibility." He starts to look around in all directions and then he says to Maury, "Gee, where did Joshua go? He was here a second ago, wasn't he?" This is Tony's favorite activity, except for complaining about his leg.

"I don't know," says Maury, grimly going along with Tony's ploy. "We were just talking to him, weren't we? I think maybe the earth swallowed him up. That happens to people sometimes."

"If he'd told the truth instead of lying all the time, then maybe this wouldn't have happened," says Tony.

According to my aunt and uncles, I'm too skinny. If I ate more, I'd be healthier and I wouldn't lie. And whenever I say something they don't like, they pull this Cloak of Invisibility schtick on me. The dumbest trick in the book, but it works on me for some reason, and I feel myself slipping away, actually becoming invisible. I tell myself, "You're not five years old, Josh. Don't let them ruffle you." But their combined wills are invincible. In the end they always succeed in snuffing me out.

Everything I've said is true, and more. I'm incapable of lying. All that stuff with Billy really happened. But the only things Maury and Tony believe are what my parents admitted, which wasn't much, because they're ashamed. Mom and Dad mentioned I was flunking out of school before, but neglected to add that I was also breaking into the neighbor's apartments and stealing stereo equipment. The last time I spoke with my Dad, who's a prof at Columbia, he said, "I don't want you to think I'm carrying a tally sheet around with me. It's all *tabula rosa* as far as I'm concerned."

He can't impress me with Latin. I know what *tabula rasa* means, and I don't want to become an empty slate.

"I *am* telling the truth," I say to Tony. "When are you going to start believing me?"

"I heard a faint voice just then," he says.

"Maybe it was Joshua," says Maury. "No, it couldn't have been. He's gone. Poof. Just like that."

"I'm right here," I say. "Will you stop it already?"

"Oh Joshua?" says Tony. "Where are you?" And then he looks at Maury and says with an unusual amount of sincerity, "It's such a shame. For a while, he seemed to be on the right track."

"The old straight and narrow," says Maury, nodding.

"I'm sorry, I'm sorry," I say. "I don't take heroin. Never have, never will."

"Look, over there!" Tony yells, pointing to me. "I see the faint outline of someone. It's getting clearer. No, it's fading now."

"Could it have been Joshua?" Maury says.

"I'm sorry," I say again. "I don't even know anyone named Billy, and I just heard that other stuff on TV."

"Joshua!" says Maury, and he smiles at me. "Welcome back." When Maury smiles, which is rare, he never smiles for long. The filbert shell of his face just cracks open for a second, and you catch a glimpse of this little square of white nut meat inside.

Tony doesn't smile at all. Instead he gives his brother a bitter look and says, "He could have stood a little more," and then starts rubbing the calf of his bum leg.

"What's that you've got in your ear, Joshua?" Rose says as soon as she sees me. Her voice is very thick and dull so she always sounds like she's chewing some tough piece of meat.

She's sitting by the pool in a deck chair. "Come here, Joshua," she says, and I dutifully go over to find out how she wants to torment me.

As soon as I'm a foot away she says, "Come closer, Joshua." Now I'm kneeling before the chair like a knight about to be dubbed. She grabs my earring and yanks it towards her. Of course my head follows along though she hardly seems to notice. "Let me see this," she says after she's pulled me halfway on top of her. With one hand, she keeps a firm hold of the earring and with the other she roots in her purse, which is the size and approximate shape of an armadillo. She pulls a pair of glasses from her purse and puts them on. Now that her hand is free again, she scrapes my earring with her thumbnail.

"What kind of metal is this?" she says. "It looks like an alloy. I've heard some alloys can give you depressions."

With that, she lets go of me.

"Have you seen Lenny?" I say. "He said he was going to take a swim."

"I'd give him a wide berth, if I were you," says

Rose. "His stability is strongly in doubt. He told me once that he smokes pot."

"When was that?"

"Oh, I don't know. It must have been nine or ten years ago. But it's something that's burned itself into my memory, and I don't want you to get any ideas from him."

"I have my own ideas," I tell her.

"I know you do," she says, patting my hand, and then adds, "Tell me, Joshua, what do *you* want to do with your life?"

I've thought about this before, so it's easy. "I want to be a musician," I say. "I want to travel back in time to the Cro-Magnon Age and be the first musician before recorded history. I'd like to bang two rocks together and create fire and then electricity and then feedback. Scream, stomp, bash. Scream, stomp, bash," and I walk around Rose's deck chair like a caveman, beating my fists together. Then I stop and add, "If not that, then I'd like to be the first graffiti artist. You know, spray-painting those pterodactyls as they fly by."

Rose looks confused, but she sticks her hand back into her pocketbook. "Here," she says. "I have something for you if you promise you won't end up like Lenny."

Two of the guests here are playing ping pong, and the ball has been traveling at a steady rate between them for what seems like at least half an hour. "The great thing," one says to the other, "is that you never sweat out here."

"What are you going to give me?" I say as she's ferreting around.

"How does twenty dollars sound?" Then she says, "But only if you promise."

"Sure," I say and just stand there.

Rose screams and takes her hand out of her pocket-book. Her hand is covered with a thick and grainy orange substance. "Look at my hands," she says, using the plural and holding both up for everyone to see, though only one is coated with the orange film. "What is this on my hands?" she says again, raising them higher, as though making a plea to heaven. "There's something on my hands. I think my pills have melted."

I don't have all day to wait around. I can feel myself going crazier by the moment in this atmosphere. Maybe Lenny can help get me out of here. At the very least, it'll be good just to talk to someone halfway sane. So I grab Rose's pocketbook off her lap and reach inside. I take out her coin purse, snap it open, and there's a twenty-dollar bill crunched on top of a bunch of loose change.

"Thanks, Rose," I tell her and head off.

The curtains are drawn across the glass door of Lenny's room. I knock on it loudly and say, "It's Josh. Save me from the barbarian hordes. Please."

Lenny slides the door open and stands there. "What are you babbling about?" he says. He looks like he just woke up. His long hair is smashed against one side of his face, and he has a dull look in his eyes. He's wearing running shorts and a T-shirt. Even though he's pretty old, at least thirty-five, everything except for his hair style makes him look younger. He's tan and tall, and he's slender but not skinny like me. His muscles are tight and well defined, not flabby like Maury's and the others'. He stays young because he does what he wants, and he's always open to new things. I'm the only one in the family who doesn't criticize him.

131

Lenny yawns, bends down, and picks up a brick-red Spalding ball lying at his feet. He starts squeezing it, and finally he says in a halfway friendly voice, "What's that in your ear?"

"Everyone's been asking me that," I say, and I step inside.

I flop down on his bed. I turn my head completely to one side of the room and then completely the other way. It's only a habit of mine now, but when I was younger I used to make believe that my eyes invented everything I saw. I had this theory that things existed only as long as I was looking at them. In reality the earth was completely formless, and I was a robot who'd been brainwashed and set down on it for the insidious purpose of some higher life forms. This was an experiment. They wanted to see how long it would take for me to catch on to their games or else go completely bonkers. When I heard my parents talking in their bedroom at night about what to do with me, they weren't really there. They were just two recordings being played in an infinite tape loop. Once I flung open their door, sure I'd find the room completely empty. I heard them jump up, but since the room was dark, it took my eyes a few seconds to actually see them. And for those moments I believed it might be true. The room contained just a couple of dark shapes I'd invented to be my parents.

"What's going on, Josh?" my father said. "You scared the daylights out of us."

I couldn't answer them at all. I just stared at them, and then I started shaking and couldn't stop. My mother had to take me to the kitchen and fix me a cup of Sleepytime tea, and she had to hold it for me because I was trembling too hard.

After that I stopped pretending.

Lenny's sitting in a chair by the dresser. He's looking at me like he expects me to say something. Maybe he'll read my mind or will know instinctively that I'm in exile.

"That's the sound of men working on the chain gaa yaa yang," I sing out.

He just gives me a look.

"Hey," I say. "Remember the time when I was a kid, and we were all sitting out on the porch at Grandma's? Someone said something that hurt my feelings, and I ran inside crying. You brought me back outside and made everyone apologize. I was always glad you did that."

"Must've been somebody else," he says.

"Here, throw me the ball."

I make a mitt out of my hands and look at him expectantly. But he throws the ball to my right. It bounces off the wall, thuds on the carpet, and rolls to a stop a yard away from his feet. He bends down to scoop it up and tries again. This time he throws the ball hard with a sidearm toss, and the Spalding glances off the wall and shoots right back to him.

"I really hate them all," I say. "Will you throw me the ball, please?"

He laughs and says, "Them? They're just harmless fleabags. It would break their hearts if they thought you hated them." He pauses and then says, "Don't tell them I called them fleabags."

"The ball," I say. "Throw it here."

He throws and I make a decent catch. Then I stick the ball in my mouth and taste its bitterness and dirt. "Ummmm!" I yell as loud as I can with the ball in my mouth.

Lenny gives me a disgusted look. "What'd you do that for, you stupid kid?"

133

I take the ball out of my mouth and smile sweetly. "I don't know. Want it back?"

"Take a guess."

"It's just that I'm going nuts around them," I say. "They're always criticizing me for the wrong things. They think I'm a liar just because I've had more experiences than they've ever had in the seven hundred and eighty years between them."

"So?" He gets this strange look on his face, the corner of his mouth going up like he's either about to smile or sneeze. "Don't let them tell you who you are. It's all a matter of believing in yourself and focusing."

"Focusing?"

"Yeah. Focus. Just pretend you're a lens, like in a camera. Let's say you see this lady across the room at some party. All you have to do is put on your telephoto lens, and zip, she's yours. It works the same with anything you want. You've got to learn how to obscure distance. It's all a matter of your field of vision. That's how I got into music. And if you want some room to breathe, then all you've got to do is put on your fish-eye lens, and bam, everyone backs off." His eyes widen suddenly for no apparent reason, and he stares at me. This sort of gives me the creeps.

Finally he blinks and says, "Focus."

"Yeah, I get it," I say. "Want to get high?"

"That's antifocus," he says, annoyed. "People always think I indulge because of this," and he lifts up the flat side of his hair and then lets it fall back in place. "Actually, I haven't indulged in over eight years. I don't care much for indulgent people these days. They're so . . ." and he searches for a word.

"Hedonistic?"

"Yeah, sort of," he says. "But I prefer a less scientific word than that. I think words are sacred. That's why I spend so much time with them when I'm writing songs." He pauses and looks hard at me.

"So you don't do *any* drugs?"

"People make false assumptions," he says, "based on selective observations."

I laugh and say, "That's a heavy rap to lay on you, man."

"You've got a big mouth," he says.

"I know. It's always getting me in trouble," and I smile to show him that I'm fully aware of and content with the meanness of my spirit.

"You're a weird kid. A little spooked-out and stuff."

"I know," I say, still pleased with myself.

But Lenny's not paying attention. He opens a drawer in the dresser without a word and takes out a pair of scissors. I walk over and say, "What are you doing?"

"It's part of the deal," he says. "I've got some plans. I want to get some new equipment and go on the road again, but I need at least three grand. I knew Maury was loaded. After all, he's footing the bill for you. So I asked him, and he told me to cut my hair first and then we'd talk about it. It took my last cent just getting here from L.A."

"I could give you a great style," I tell him. "Do you have a razor? We could cut your hair real short in the back except for one really thin long strip. Then we could shave the sides about three inches above the ears in a crescent. We'd leave it long in the front."

"I don't want to look like a freak," he says.

He looks at himself in the mirror and makes a tentative chop at some hair near his shoulders. But instead of cutting across he yanks the scissors downward like a comb and succeeds only in pulling out a few long blond strands.

135

"That hurt," he says.

"Of course it hurt," I say. "If everyone cut hair like that it would take them forever and they'd wind up bald."

"I was just seeing how it felt," he says. A moment later he begins in earnest. He starts on the right, choosing a spot halfway up his face, and cuts across the hair as he looks at himself in the mirror. Even though he looks like he hasn't had his hair cut since the 60's he handles the scissors like a pro, grabbing tufts and pulling until they're even before cutting them away. In a few minutes, all his hair except the very back is page-boy length. He can't reach there, so I say, "It looks like you need some help."

He doesn't pay attention to my offer, but instead bends down and starts to chop away at the back.

"You know what hair is?" he says. "It's just a waste product from your scalp. Having a full head of hair is like carrying around a bunch of crap in your pants. It's weird that people even bother."

This thought disturbs me, so I go over to him and say, "Here, let me. You don't know what you're doing."

"Keep away," he says, and a big clump falls to the floor. "It's my hair. You want to wipe my ass too?"

"I just wanted to help," I say, but too soft to hear.

He looks in the mirror and says, "What do you think?" but I'm not sure he's asking me. He picks up his scissors again and says, "I'd say that was about two thousand dollars worth." Then he grabs the lock of hair over his forehead and holds the scissors across it like some kidnapper threatening the life of a hostage.

"Please, please!" he yells in a squeaky voice. "Let me go. We can work out a deal. I have a rich wig. He'll give you a lifetime supply of combs. Anything!"

Then he cuts the lock away.

136

Now that his hair is a lot shorter I notice something. The shape of his head looks just like a bullet. His chin is flat and square, and there's a thickness to the sides of his face, coming to a slight point at the top.

I turn my back on him, walk to the window, and open the curtains.

"You need some air in here," I say. "Do you always live like this?"

Looking out the window, I forget where I am for a moment. The door to one of the saunas opens and a bunch of steam flows out. I imagine that it expands until steam covers everything. People are shrinking, losing weight at an incredible pace in this miracle sauna of ours. The earth is returning to its gaseous state.

When I turn around again, Lenny's at the table smiling at me.

"You know," he says. "I hate them too. Better watch out you don't wind up like them, wasting your life at some stupid motor lodge in the desert. You must be bored to tears."

"You should see how you look," I reply. "You look totally bizarre."

"I'm not done yet," he says, putting down his scissors and walking over to me.

"I wouldn't have had to do any of this if not for you," he says. "Maury's helped me out before, without conditions. All of a sudden you show up, and the hair comes off."

"Sorry to cause you grief," I say.

"I would have done it differently," he says. "I would have put you in some boys' home instead of bringing you out here. From what I hear you're uncontrollable," and then he puts his hand on my neck and squeezes the way he was squeezing the Spalding ball before, with a slight pumping motion. Even though he does this for only a second, I blank out. When I open my eyes again, all I can think about are the invisible scars he's left on my neck. I can't believe someone can just come up and do that to me. If he was completely crazy he'd keep squeezing and there'd be nothing I could do. For a moment I see everyone I know trying to choke the life out of each other.

"I don't see what's so special about you," Lenny says, going to his bed and sitting down. He looks at me and smiles, which shocks me even more. He doesn't seem to realize that squeezing someone's neck isn't considered a friendly gesture by most people.

I take out an imaginary sword and parry an opponent's thrust and then stab out in Lenny's direction.

Lenny just keeps on smiling. "Why don't you put in a good word for me with Maury? I need your help. He's got this wrong impression of me."

"I'm not going to help you," I tell him.

"Sure you will. He's under your spell," and he winks at me.

I think about this a moment and say, "Okay, I'll see what I can do."

With that, I head for my room. When I'm inside, I pull out the last remnants of the bag I brought from New York.

I was actually saving it for a special occasion, but this will do. Quickly I roll a joint and grab a pack of matches from the night table. I light it on the way to the main courtyard. Maury, Tony, and Rose are all sitting around the pool with their eyes closed, catching the last rays of the sun.

I take a few hits and then sit down next to Maury. Already I've got the attention of about half the guests in the place.

"Lenny gave this to me," I tell Maury. "Want some?" and I hand the joint to him.

Reflexively he takes it from me. A moment later he opens his eyes wide.

I'm under the influence now, feeling drowsy and good about things. I help Lenny. Lenny helps me. Even Houdini needs an assistant when he's struggling under-water. *Someone's* got to stand there looking pretty as the seconds ring out in his waterlogged ears. Hold up that handcuff key, honey. That's right, let everybody see.

After dinner, the four of us sit around the lounge. My unfortunate cousin has left us, though not before causing quite a stir at the old Ma-Ho-Pa Spa. You should have seen Maury and Tony storm into his room with loud denunciations of pot and the corrupting influence of a musician's life. Lenny left in a hurry, with only half a haircut and much less than three grand in his pocket. Fifty bucks to make it back to L.A. "Never darken the Brewer doorstep again," Maury told him. Those were his exact words.

And now that Lenny has departed, the four of us are having the time of our lives. Rose offers me a sip of her margarita and I taste it gingerly, as though I've never had one. I even make a face as though it tastes awful. Everyone laughs and Maury says, "I remember the first time you ate an oyster. Your eyes stuck out halfway from your head. You didn't want to swallow it, but you didn't want to spit it out either. How old were you then?"

"Nine."

"Nine. How old are you now?"

My name is Joshua Brewer. I am fifteen years old.

"Fifteen," he says and shakes his head.

Then the band strikes up some Xavier Cougat, and I feel like dancing. At some point every evening this band plays Xavier Cougat, though I've never wanted to move to it before. I ask Rose if she wants to dance. She laughs and swats the air, so I get up alone and go through the motions, like a sloppy flamenco dancer with a hand on my stomach and my other hand in the air, even though you aren't supposed to do flamenco to Xavier Cougat.

As I'm dancing I touch my hand to my earlobe. The ear feels infected and I can imagine how it looks, inflamed and puffy. So I remove the earring and hold it in my hand.

Now Tony gets up and starts doing some weird tango. He seems to have forgotten all about his bum leg. Rose and Maury get up too and do a fox trot together. Then we join in a line and start doing a chain dance, grinding our hips and kicking our legs out with perfect timing, first one side and then the other. We're all dancing now, all the barbarian hordes snaking across the land, taking things over, setting the trends, making the rules, and building our dynasty outward from all the mineral spas and deserts in the country.

Rainwalkers

Your head is bent against the rain, droplets beading on your chin, and you're not thinking about much. Not Julia or getting home, or even the chill you feel through your clothes. Julia, if she was here, would ask what's wrong. To her, silence is a condemnation. She wants incessant talk, and not only from you, but from the radio, the TV, and her two cats, whom she constantly prods with meows. While making love, she stops and asks why you're so silent. If you spend too long in the bathroom, she knocks and says, "You haven't flushed yourself down the pipes, have you?"

Tonight Julia is luxuriating. A bubble bath, a magazine, and a gin and tonic. Every light's on in the house, the stereo plays Windham Hill. Her bubble bath scent is steaming out of a crack in the bathroom door. If your apartment had a taste, it would be purple sourball.

So you've slipped out. You don't care if it's raining. Let it rain. But you're not angry with Julia. When she can't get what she needs from you, she soaks in the tub and lets her essence spread through the apartment, filling all its corners like weatherproofing caulk.

Walking fast, you think of the hours Julia wastes getting waterlogged in the tub. Maybe it wasn't such a good idea moving in with her. You both could have used more time. "Where's the fire?" you said when she suggested the arrangement after only three months.

ROBIN HEMLEY

The rain's drumming soon slows your pace. You notice a tilted hitching post, made to look like a horse's head, water dripping from its nostrils. You run your hand along a black iron fence that surrounds a Victorian house you've always admired. You notice the overhanging trees, the occasional car slipping by. When you're in this rain-induced state, you look at cars the way animals must. You focus on the lights shuddering in their path, not on the people inside, but the territorial whine of the engine and tires. When the car passes, you're a dumb animal again, splashing ahead without purpose, succored by the sound of the gutters filling in the street. A Styrofoam cup swirls past. A loaf of Roman Meal bread, still in its wrapper, sags on the sidewalk. A true walker in the rain doesn't pause too long at this sight. A novice might step on it or give it a kick. A professional just keeps walking, making his little splashings until he's made enough.

You walk at least twenty blocks before turning around, a little disappointed because you feel you could walk the length of the city this night. On your way back, you try to forget you're heading home.

The rain is letting up. Some people who were caught when the downpour started now emerge from awnings and doorways, rushing past with newspapers or bags over the tops of their heads. A couple of taxis skulk down the road, and a kid riding a bicycle with a banana seat and fat tires blocks the way at one corner, balanced on a wheel, and then twirls around with a skid. You pass him quickly. Now you want to reach home before the rain ends so your illusion won't be completely broken.

A half block away from the apartment, a woman walks towards you. Like you, she doesn't have an umbrella and she isn't wearing a coat. Her long blonde hair

142

is matted against the sides of her face, and she walks slowly, her head bent down.

Not too unusual. Just another rainwalker.

She's carrying something, toting it along with one arm, like a tired child dragging home a favorite doll. From a distance, it looks like a gas cannister. As you move closer, you see it's a fire extinguisher, a big one, the kind you'd find in a movie theater or an office building.

Almost nothing needs an explanation in the rain. A package of Roman Meal bread, a Styrofoam cup, a car on its way somewhere. You don't need to know where the car is going, who drank from the cup, or whether someone dropped the loaf of bread out of a disintegrating grocery bag while rushing home in the downpour.

But a woman carrying a fire extinguisher in the rain? As she approaches, you remember the well-dressed man striding down the street the other day, his face a hideous red, his fists balled at his sides, and bellowing at thirty-second intervals like a bull. The schizophrenics strung out like dropped change jostle your thoughts on your way to work each morning. But you expect that. You're already agitated, not enough sleep, an argument, you forgot something at home. The whole world's blighted, and you wish you could do something for these people. The hospitals are teeming. Thank God you're normal. What a horrible life it must be to bellow like a bull at thirty-second intervals.

Your holy rainwalks are different. You're different. Someone walking past with an umbrella, one of the dry ones, might mistake you for a homeless person, or at least think you've slipped a cog. But you don't care. To a rainwalker, it's acceptable to be unacceptable. That's part of the rain's attraction.

Okay, you think. You can accept a woman carrying

a fire extinguisher in the rain. You can accept anything. But you slow down a bit to see as much of her as possible before you pass each other. She wears high heels and a black dress and has earrings on, too. She doesn't look homeless. She looks like a party-goer, an eater in restaurants, a taxi-rider, a watcher of the weatherman's charts and cardboard cumuli, one of the multitude of people who don't like to get wet.

You try to avoid her eyes. You don't want to alarm her, but she doesn't even seem to notice you.

After you've gone five feet or so, you have a feeling and turn around. She's turned around, too, and is staring at you. Slowly you walk a little closer and say, "Is anything wrong?"

"Were you whistling at me?" she says.

"Whistling?" you say, a bit flustered. "I was just on my way home. I live right here. Maybe I was whistling, but not at you. I like to go for walks in the rain, and sometimes I do things I'm not even conscious of."

She looks a little suspicious. "You didn't go like this?" and she whistles.

"Sorry, must have been someone else."

"Oh, I thought it was you."

You smile and start to walk away.

"I sometimes do things I'm not conscious of," she says.

"I guess we all do," you say.

The woman heaves the fire extinguisher into her arms and shifts her weight. She looks tired, and you wonder why she doesn't just put the thing down.

"Nice chatting," you say. "Long day tomorrow."

"We get an extra hour," she says. "Do you know what you're going to do with yours?"

"Probably fly to Aruba and get a little sun. I guess I'll just wait and see what happens."

"When's your birthday?" she says.

An astrologist. "I don't know, a couple of months from now," you say.

She laughs. "You don't know when your birthday is?"

"Sure I know, I'm just tired."

"My boyfriend has a birthday tomorrow," she says. "He was born at two in the morning, but it's really one in the morning because of the time change. That's always bothered him. It's almost like being born on a leap year."

"I think I'll go inside now," you say. "You should probably do the same. Don't want to come down with anything."

The woman looks as though she's waiting for something else. Does she want to be invited inside? A stray cat or dog you might get away with, but Julia would have a fit if you brought home a sopping woman with a fire extinguisher.

You're wet and miserable. You don't know what you're doing talking to her. Maybe she has a logical reason for carrying it around, but maybe she doesn't. You're scared to ask. You never know. She might squirt you with the thing. You like to think of yourself as an accepting kind of person. Everyone has quirks. Some people soak in the bathtub for hours. Others walk in the rain without an umbrella. But you do this because you like it. For relaxation. You can't say that someone walking in the rain with a fire extinguisher enjoys dragging the thing around. On the other hand, you've come down with some terrible colds from these walks, and Julia knows she's soaking away all her precious body oils. You could spend your lifetime trying to explain why you walk around in thunderstorms and still never get to the bottom of it.

"I hope it stops raining before Tony's birthday," the

woman says. "He hates the rain. Actually, he hates any kind of bad weather. Or anything, for that matter, that's out of his control. Hurricanes, earthquakes. He woke me up one night and said that the bed was trembling. I couldn't feel anything, but he made me dress, and we stood out in the middle of the street for an hour until he was sure it was safe again."

The woman shifts the weight of her fire extinguisher and brushes back a little hair from her eyes. "He thinks I'm making fun of him," she says. "Do you think people are afraid to live without their fears?" she adds, her voice strong, her eyes suddenly bright.

To anyone passing by, this is probably a mystifying sight, two people huddled in the rain, a tall man listening to a short woman carrying a fire extinguisher. Maybe they think that the two of you live together in the building you're standing in front of. There was a fire in your apartment, and you called the fire department and then tried to put the fire out yourselves. But it wouldn't go out. And so you fled into the rain, with no time to bring anything valuable, except for the very thing that failed to save you.

But no one passes, although who knows if anyone is watching from inside.

"Sandra? Do you see those two people standing out there in the rain. I think one of them is carrying a torpedo."

"It's probably just a lovers' quarrel. Leave them alone."

"A quarrel with a torpedo? There might be violence. Maybe we should call the police or the bomb squad."

The woman with the fire extinguisher breaks into your thoughts.

"I know it must look silly," she says, "but that's the reason."

"The reason?"

"The fire extinguisher. I know it looks stupid. People have been crossing the street all night. You were the first person who stopped. I guess I just needed to talk. I think I'll go home now. Tony's probably not angry anymore."

The rain starts up again in loud torrents.

"Wait a minute," you shout. "I wasn't paying attention. Don't go away."

Apparently she doesn't hear. She keeps walking. A moment later she stops, and you think she might come back and finish the conversation. But she doesn't. She just bends down and places the fire extinguisher on the sidewalk. She rests it gently, as though it's some animal that's died in her arms.

Standing up, she covers her head with her hands and runs away through the downpour.

Slowly you walk over to the fire extinguisher and examine it. You turn it over. A card is attached. You can't read the names or the message because the rain has washed the ink away. All you know for sure is that it's a birthday card.

You throw the card back down and look off in the direction the woman's run. You leave the fire extinguisher where it lies.

You want the woman to return and continue her rainwalk. This confrontation breaks all your traditions, but you want her to come back and tell you more.

When you return to the apartment, Julia is still in the tub. You stand outside the bathroom door and say, "You haven't gone down the drain have you?"

No answer, and you have the image of Julia completely submerged in her bubble bath, her gin and tonic knocked over into the tub with her. People have drowned in an inch before, even less. She's fallen asleep in the tub twice that you know of, once only a week ago. You're always reminding her to stay awake, or at least not to drink while she's soaking. But she says that the tub is the only place she enjoys drinking.

You knock on the door. "Julia, are you all right in there?"

"I'm fine," she says. "I must have fallen asleep. I wasn't even aware of it."

"My God, Julia. You should lay off the juice while you're in the tub at least. Next time I might not be around. In fact, I was out walking. I just got home."

"Home?" she says. "I didn't know you were gone. I hope you took an umbrella this time."

"The rain's stopped. I didn't need an umbrella."

"It's been absolutely pouring," she says. "I could hear it in here."

You don't answer. You feel a sneeze coming on. You open your mouth, but then you hold your nose to stifle it.

Water sloshes as though she's stood up.

"Long day tomorrow," you say.

Now she's drying herself off and putting on her bathrobe.

"That reminds me," she says. "We should set the clocks back."

You don't want her to come out, to see her just yet. You want to get out of your wet clothes.

"You can stay in there if you want," you say. "I can set the clocks back."

She pauses. "I might as well come out. My drink needs freshening, and I'm starting to feel like a jellyfish."

"Don't bother," you say, "I'll make it a double. Relax. Enjoy yourself."

148

Rainwalkers

"You're a dear," she says. After a moment, you hear her settle back in the tub.

"Could you turn over my record, too?"

You nod yes, even though you know Julia can't see you. Your walk has tired you out. You put your head against the door. You probably look like a doctor listening to the faltering beat of a patient.

There's a lock on the bathroom door. You can't remember ever seeing it though you're sure it's always been there. Why would anyone want to lock a bathroom from the outside? Maybe the people who lived here before kept pets inside.

Without thinking about what you're doing or why, you flip the lock in place. You listen to Julia splashing around in there.

Then you think about that extra hour tomorrow. What will you do with it? You wish the time change were today. You could use that extra hour. The rain is already stopping, and tomorrow night will probably be clear. You feel a fever coming on, and the small delirious pleasure of not being able to focus. How nice always to be in this state, never to know what you're doing or why. You almost *need* to come down with something, to be really sick, to doubt whether or not you're going to make it.

Installations

One of the first things the group did was to engage its film maker-associate Ken Kobland to shoot the beautiful surrealistic movie that concludes the piece. In the film, Mr. Vawter, outfitted in Arabic-bohemian garb, prods the flesh of an elderly dead woman with his walking stick.
　　　　　　—Stephen Holden in *The New York Times*

　　　　　　　　　Finding things. That's what I love most about my job. Over the last ten years, I've found money, rings, wallets, knives, a couple of guns, umbrellas, pens, watches. Weird little statues. I have three Buddhas sitting at home, and a big African ebony thing with an hourglass in the middle.

A lot of things you wouldn't believe. A piece or two of men's or women's underwear almost every week, sometimes fresh, more often soiled. At 2 a.m., a cigarette lighter made out of a hand grenade rolls around in the middle of the car. No one even notices, or if they do, they just think, "Someone's dumb idea of a joke," and go back to sleep or look out the window, daring the thing to explode. After all, these people ride the El everyday. They've been around the block a few times. So have I. Some people would pull the emergency brake and yell, "Run for the hills!" But you can't phase *me.* Instead, I pick up the pineapple, see it's just a lighter, and stow it in my conductor's jacket. Now it sits on my coffee table at home.

150

Installations

Of course, I'm not supposed to keep anything I find. Regulations state you're supposed to turn everything in to Lost and Found.

Yeah, right.

*A*t rush hour, a guy wearing polyester pants with a pattern that looks like chain mail steps onto my car. A frilly straw hat covers his head, but I notice him because he's plastered with kooky buttons all over his chest like some Soviet field marshal. The buttons have sayings on them: "Are We Having Fun Yet?" "Instant Asshole . . . Just Add Alcohol," "Wake Me Up, I'm A Lot Of Fun," "Trust Me, I'm A Doctor," "Dain Bramaged," "Hallucination Now In Progress. Please Stand By," "Ask Me If I Care," "I'm The Person Your Mother Warned You About," and "Born Again Pagan."

A little guy with half yellow and half black hair accompanies the button man. An army poncho hangs from his shoulders and a cigarette sits behind his ear. He looks faithful but bored, like the bodyguard of a low-level dignitary, and carries a book with a strange title, *Utopia TV Store.*

"It took me thirty-five years to overcome my disease," the button man tells me, "but I did it."

"That's good," I say. No big surprise that he wants to talk to me. I come from a family of authority figures. My Uncle Jerry's a priest and you can see my brother Ted on billboards all over the 'burbs. He's the model for Captain Safety Belt, wearing a hat like mine and two seat belts criss-crossed like bandoliers on his chest. I've dealt with plenty of people like the button man, people who latch onto the conductor because he's the Cardinal

Bernardin of the rush hour chaos. They're always holding forth to me about something or other. The camera that follows them around their apartment. Or how they saw the Holy Ghost pissing on the station escalators.

"I learned how to make buttons all by myself," says the man. "No one showed me how."

"That's nice," I say.

I lean into the intercom and announce, "No smoking, littering, or radio playing allowed. Clark and Division will be next. Clark and Division." I run those words together, and emphasize the "Vision" so it becomes ClarkandiVISION, like I'm announcing some spectacular new movie technique. Filmed in Technicolor, Panavision, and introducing . . . ClarkandiVISION. What does it look like? Narrow and dark. The way things look when you're speeding through a tunnel. A couple of loons get on, you say, "Roll 'em." The doors close, the loons leave, you say, "Cut, that's a wrap."

The commuters stand in their defense stances, like people in a kung fu movie waiting for the hero to unleash his awesome power. They eye the button man warily while holding onto the seats and bars to keep from falling.

I'm sure in the next ten minutes I'll learn all about the button man's life, how he's overcome his disease and found sanctuary in the world of buttons.

"I'm a writer," the button man tells me. "I'm writing a novel right now about my experience, and I've also got a hundred poems about my disease. My novel's going to be called, *In It To Win*. That's because I stayed in it for thirty-five years and now I'm winning."

"That's nice," I say. The guy looks his age, which is remarkable for a loon. Most of them look about twice their actual age. Yesterday, a guy told me the Shriners had vowed to make an example of him before his

152

twenty-first birthday. (I've dealt with other people who think The Mooses, The Elks, or The Lions Club is trying to hunt them down. I wonder if they freak out every time they see a donation box by a cash register). The kid looked to be late thirties, but then I saw he was still a teenager like he said, that the lines in his face were from lack of sleep, not age.

I'm younger than the button man, but I look almost forty. My hairline is eroding faster than the beach in front of some North Shore condo. My mustache is turning grey. My voice is losing its authority, becoming thinner. And my toenails have curled and yellowed like old people's. A couple of weeks ago, I found something on my big toe, and two of my friends told me it was a bunion. A bunion! I didn't think the word even entered your vocabulary until you were eighty. Presidents aren't the only ones who age in office. Conductors, too.

As we make the brake-screeching turn to Clark and Division, the button man's yellow-and-black-haired friend drops his book at my feet. I wait for him to retrieve it, but he acts like it's just some litter he's not going to bother with.

"A movie company is going to interview me tomorrow," the button man says. "They want to do a video on me. In a little while *The Sun-Times* is going to do a story about me and my disease. Maybe not today or tomorrow, but soon. I'm that confident. I'm hot. Isn't that right, Gus?" and he nudges his buddy. "The *Sun-Times* is going to do a story on me."

"That's right," says Gus.

"He always agrees with me," says the button man and laughs.

We unload some people at Clark and Division and head off.

"It took thirty-five years out of my life."

"That's too bad," I say.

The button man starts making funny noises. "Coo Coo Coodle Coo," he sings.

After a few choruses, the button man stops abruptly, looks out the window, and shouts, "We're talking schizophrenia here." The commuters near him scoot away and look down their chests.

"This wasn't a good idea to take the El," the button man tells his friend. "Remind me never to take it again. It's too claustrophobic. It's counterproductive, and you know how I feel about things that are counterproductive."

"That's right," says his friend.

"Let's get some more buttons, Gus," the button man tells his friend. "I feel like some more buttons. How 'bout you, Gus?"

"Whatever you say," says Gus, and they both get off the car at Fullerton.

I'm a little sorry to see them go. People like them make the job interesting. I try my best to sympathize. You have to make these people feel appreciated. They lead rough lives, and besides, they're the CTA's most frequent riders.

We start up again. Gus has left his book behind. Each page has a little paragraph with titles like, "Kill Yourself With an Objet D'art" and "A Vegetable Emergency." I try figuring out a few paragraphs, but they don't make any sense. I'll turn it in to the Lost and Found.

Then, at Belmont, a girl about twenty flings herself at me and yells, "A prose poem fan. A kindred spirit."

At first, I'm thinking, "Great, another live one." She starts jabbering about the book in my hand. I'm about to tell her I just found it on the floor, but then I figure there's no harm in letting her talk. She's a runt: skinny with no hips and nubby breasts. Her hair's black, short, and tufted like a boy's. But she's quick to smile and laugh, and she locks her eyes on me. A uniform freak, I figure.

Her name is Ivy, and she's from a small town about ten miles south of Beloit, Wisconsin. "Cody, Illinois," she says. "The Beefalo capital of the Midwest." She's twenty-one, a student at The Art Institute, where she's studying performance art.

"You mean like musicals?"

She laughs and says, "I mean like The Wooster Group, or Michael Meyers or Ethel Eichelberger or David Cale or John Kelly —"

"Never heard of them," I say and get up to announce the next station and open the doors.

When I return, she says, "Then you've probably heard of —" She pauses, puts a hand to her chest, and leans forward. "Laurie Anderson." She says this as though she's really saying, "Hemorrhoids." "Personally," she continues, "I'd rather see *Beatlemania* or a strobe light flickering for forty-eight hours."

If you know what she's talking about, you've got me beat. But I pretend to understand her anyway, just like I did with the button man.

Ivy leans forward again. "Don't you think the El would be an ingenious place for an installation?"

"Yeah, right," I say, "but not until they fix the air conditioners."

We sit across from each other. Ivy huddles close to me, her eyes bright, and says, "I can be your accomplice."

"Sounds great," I say.

She tells me one weird story after another. A man and a woman are tied together by a three foot rope for a year. By choice. They have to follow each other everywhere. Even to the john. And they hardly knew each other before they tied the knot, so to speak. Of course, I know people who get into that sort of thing. Bondage. But Ivy shakes her head and says, "You're completely wrong and absolutely right. It's bondage of a different sort. They're making a statement about the bondage of male/female role-playing. And on the positive side, they're saying that the male and female parts of everyone are inextricably bound. The more we try to escape from the Other, the closer he/she follows."

Yeah, right.

*W*hen my shift is up, Ivy gets off with me at my stop. She seems completely oblivious to the fact that we've gotten off the train. She just keeps walking beside me and talking. Asking questions. Most of them she answers herself. I haven't figured her game yet, but I don't mind her tagging along.

I live in Wrigleyville, on Cornelia, a block from the Friendly Confines. That's my favorite neighborhood in the city. The best thing is summer. Sometimes I walk out on my back porch, and hear the national anthem shimmering from the park. You can't help but feel you're in a dream when you're doing something really ordinary, like taking a load of laundry down to the laundry room, and all of a sudden there's "The Star-Spangled Banner." Not to mention when

156

you're sitting on the pot and a cheer of thirty thousand people comes out of nowhere. It makes you tingle. You feel like you're a part of something. Sometimes, when I hear the anthem or a cheer I drop whatever I'm doing, head over to Wrigley Field, and see if the scalpers have an extra bleacher ticket. Then I zone out in the right field bleachers for the rest of the day, drinking Old Style, getting a red nose from the sun, and yelling and screaming at the left field bleachers, "Left field sucks! Left field sucks!" One day, the Mets are in town, and Strawberry rocks one right to me. Naturally, I want to make this part of my memorabilia collection, but no way with the animals around me. "Throw it back! Throw it back!" they chant, and when I hesitate, someone sloshes beer on me. So I plop the ball back on the field, and Dawson picks it up and tosses it to the side. Everyone around me cheers and the guy next to me gives me a nudge and belches. At that moment I feel like Strawberry's homer isn't worth diddly-squat.

At my apartment, Ivy won't stay in one spot for more than five seconds. The place is a sty, but she insists on checking out every room.

"You looking for something?" I say. "You want something to drink? I've got Cuervo Gold and Old Style."

"I don't drink alcohol," she says, momentarily appearing in my bedroom door before crossing to the bathroom.

"Then all's I got is Tahitian Treat," I say, peering at the plastic liter bottle in my fridge. The only other thing to eat or drink is a two-foot-long summer sausage from Hickory Farms that my Mom bought me for my birthday. All the way in the back is my jar for Cubs tickets. I keep them there so that if the apartment burns up, it won't be a total loss. Right now, I have a ticket in the jar for Cubs Umbrella Day. It's a Dodgers game with Valenzuela pitching, but half of the reason I'm going is the free umbrella. I already have a Cubs AM/FM radio from Radio Day, a Cubs cooler from Cooler Day, and a Cubs briefcase from Briefcase Day.

"Tahitian Treat sounds luscious," she says.

I bring the drinks into the living room and start flipping through my records for something to play.

"What kind of music do you like?"

"You have any Sinatra?" she says.

"Does the Pope shit in the woods?"

I put on the album with "Witchcraft."

Ivy emerges from the bathroom and says, "I grew up with Sinatra," and walks to the couch and stands on top of it. She steps behind me to the end of the couch. I take a sip of Old Style. Ivy plops down and picks up her glass of red pop. She holds this out in front of her and says, "I never would have guessed Tahitian Treat looked like this. I've never seen anything so red, have you? Where do you think they get it from? Do you think there's a red dye mine in Tahiti? I bet the native miners have to wear dark goggles in the Treat mines."

"I guess so." I take another sip of Old Style.

"You've got a great view from your bathroom," she says.

"It's just the wall of the next building."

"You ever go to Exit or The Cubby Bear?" she says.

"No."

"You know, Vacant Yellow's at the Cubby Bear on Saturday. Vacant Yellow's a group of ex-cabbies from Boston. I saw an interview with them in *The Face* this month. Can you believe Metro advertises in *The Face*? I don't go there often. Too much techno-funk. But sometimes if you just want to bop around, it's all right. If you're tired of staring into the abyss. I was in there last weekend with a whole crowd from London. They must have seen the ad in *The Face*."

Ivy takes a sip of her Tahitian Treat, and I nod. I imagine Ivy and the London crowd bopping around in the abyss.

She puts down her glass and sits back on the couch with me.

"You have an eclectic soul, don't you?" she says. "And old."

I've just finished my shift. I'm tired. I still have my uniform on. "Old King Cole was a merry old soul and a merry old soul was he," I manage.

Apparently, that's the wrong thing. Ivy slides away and gets up from the couch. She makes a slow circuit of the room. I pick up my grenade lighter from the coffee table and toss it from one hand to another for a while. Ivy ends up by my mantle and looks at me as though she's going to start a speech. I just watch her and finish my beer.

Then she picks up one of my Cuervo Gold bottles and turns it over. I have about a hundred and eighty empty Cuervo bottles around the house, fifty of them on my mantle. "What's this?" she says. "It says, 'Cicero. Sally and Mary Siriani, July 19, 1987."

"My Cuervo collection. It's something I started doing about five years back. Every time I finish one, I put the date I drank the bottle, and who I shared it with."

She picks up another one and reads, "Sally and Mary Siriani. Wrigleyville. July 20, 1987."

"The Sirianis and me go all the way back to kindergarten."

She picks up another one and reads, "Sally and Mary. In the gutter. July 21, 1987."

Ivy puts the bottle down, wanders back to the couch, and sits down next to me again. She sits with her hands crossed on her lap and her head tilted like a tourist listening to directions.

"Tell me about them," she says.

"There's not much to tell," I say. "They're sort of the party type. Sort of wild."

"Are you sort of wild?" Ivy says.

I half-shrug. "Yeah, sort of sort of," I say. "Let me tell you how I found that hand grenade lighter. It's quite a story."

Ivy grabs my hand grenade lighter. She knocks over the glass of Tahitian Treat. Crazily, she whips the lighter across the room.

"Duck!" she yells and buries herself in my lap.

The grenade slashes through the middle of my Cuervo collection, bounces off the mantle, and thuds twice. Two of the bottles shatter right off, glass spraying everywhere. Five others topple off the mantle, three bursting on the hardwood floor. Frank coughs into a new song. The two unbroken bottles roll towards me, one stopping against a leg of the coffee table.

Ivy stays in my lap, hands over her head.

Slowly, she raises her head and opens her eyes. She looks around the room like someone emerging from a bomb shelter.

"Sort of sort of," she says.

Sometimes I believe that people aren't nearly as bizarre as they let on. I imagine a date with the button man.

I reach for my can of Old Style on the coffee table and tilt it to my mouth. Empty. One warm drop, as refreshing as sweat, trickles onto my tongue.

Installations

I'm not easy to faze, but I don't expect this kind of behavior from a girl I invite over. Not that I invited her over.

I feel like I've just spent an afternoon in the bleachers. The way you get when you've been drinking beer in the sun for three hours. Bleached out. Completely in-between. Up for anything. That's how I feel right now, watching Tahitian Treat drip down the leg of the coffee table and onto an empty Cuervo bottle.

I'm not sure exactly how this happens, but we wind up slow-dancing in the middle of the living room, which is a mess. We dance around the debris.

*I*n bed, her breath catches when I touch her, so I take my hand away. Ivy goes to sleep right off, but I lie there for a couple of hours before stammering into a rush hour dream. Too many people stand in the small space in between the cars, and I can't get near enough to latch the safety chains. One by one, they fall off as we round the corners.

*T*he next day, Ivy starts bringing stuff into the apartment. She says she's been staying in Wicker Park with some junkie friends of Phil, her ex-boyfriend. A pan of beef stroganoff she made disappeared and turned up a week later under a pile of clothes in one of her roommates' closets. And Phil stabbed her with a fork. She rolls up a sleeve and shows me four red marks, closely spaced. "Phil's a tag artist," she tells me. "A good one, too. But he's awfully volatile. Besides, the landlord showed up today with a cop, and the two of them started putting our furniture on the front steps. I asked Gem what was going on. 'What happened to the rent money I gave you?' I said. 'I don't know,' she said. 'I been paying him every month. Maybe he don't remember.' I figured I could stay with you a couple of days."

Within 36 hours of our meeting, Ivy's completely installed herself in my apartment. I'm just a bystander. I don't say yes and I don't say no. But I'm curious.

We pass through a white curtain into this scene: a darkened room with a naked man and woman, thirtyish, lying like two sticks of old butter in the middle of the room. Either they're dead or mannikins. The music in the room sounds like the part in *The Wizard of Oz* where Dorothy and her boyfriends are looking at the witch's castle, and the soldiers march around singing: "O-li-o-eyohhh-oh."

Ivy takes my hand and we approach the couple on the floor. A dozen other people saunter around as though nothing special's going on. We can't get any closer than five feet. The couple on the floor are surrounded by hundreds of apples in the shape of a cross. A ragged bat hangs above them, its ribbed wings stretching six feet. A sideways neon eight sways between the wings and glows pale blue.

This is what Ivy calls an installation. This is what I call a fun house.

Up close, I see their chests moving slightly, a small

tremor from one of the woman's fingers touching the man's hand, a flickering eyelid. I study them and wonder if I've ever seen them on the El. I wonder if the woman's parents know this is what she does for a living. The man looks a little like the button man without his buttons.

Candles burn on their chests. Luckily the candles are in jars, or the wax would be excruciating. Still, the heat must get to them. Not that I can tell. They're not exactly your liveliest couple. I can imagine showing up at Angel's Shortstop, my neighborhood bar, with them stiff as corpses on the bar stools, the candles still stuck on their chests. Angel would serve them up a couple of Old Styles, and squint at me and say, "They friends of yours?"

Yeah, they're installations.

We take the El back to Belmont and walk over to Clark Street. Everything seems strange tonight: a man waiting in the window of a tattoo parlor, the moan coming out of a storefront church.

Ivy asks me what I think about the installations. I don't know. I haven't thought about it. What are you supposed to think about a naked man and woman with candles on their chests?

"Everything," she says. "Adam and Eve lying in suspended animation beneath death and infinity. Christ figures surrounded by the forbidden fruit."

Yeah, well, I guess.

We turn the corner of Clark and Belmont, and two kids, one black and one white, not more than nine years old, slam into us as they tear through the parking lot of Dunkin' Donuts.

"Hey, watch where you're going," I say, touching the white one lightly on the shoulder.

"You watch where you're going, you fag," the kid tells me.

The black kid has a pizza box in his hands. He smiles and says, "You want some pizza?"

"Yeah, you want some pizza?" says the white kid.

The black kid opens up the box. Inside is a squirrel, its head smashed, its legs stretched out, its belly split open. At least a hundred cars have run over it. As flat as a pizza. A circle of dried tomato paste surrounds the carcass.

Before I can react, the kids run off shouting and laughing. They block one pedestrian after another yelling, "Hey, you want some pizza? Free pizza."

Ivy picks up a soft drink cup from the sidewalk and throws it after them. The cup, plastic lid and straw still attached, falls to the ground three feet away.

"You brats," she screams. "Come back here."

Ivy takes off. The white kid trips. She chases the other one. I can't make out much through the distance and pedestrians. A few minutes later, she comes smiling back with the pizza box in her hands, the lid closed.

"What do you want *that* for?" I say.

"Stealing is the most sincere form of flattery," she says. "Picasso did it. Every great artist does it."

"Throw it away."

"Are you kidding?"

"Throw it away."

"Don't give me orders. I had to fight them for it."

I don't say a word. I'm tired of her. I was curious before, but now I'm just tired. I head for Angel's Short-stop and Ivy tags along. I figure it's Ivy's turn to feel out-of-place. Not many out-of-place people ever wander

Installations

into Angel's. If they do, they wander back out again in a hurry. The crowd at Angel's is as tight as a VFW post.

Ignoring Ivy, I sit down on a stool at the bar. There isn't one for her, so she stands in between my stool and the next guy's, and places her pizza box on the counter. Angel gives her a look. Then she looks at me. I order a couple shots of Cuervo with Old Style chasers.

"I'll have to tap a new keg," says Angel. "How 'bout something else in the meantime?"

"How 'bout a mug of beefalo swill?" I say. "Come on, Angel. I'm talking brand loyalty."

"I'll go tap a new keg," she says. Angel is about sixty years old and has a white bubble hair-do. She comes to Chicago via the coal mines of Kentucky, and her husband's long-gone with black lung. Angel's jukebox has only the thickest country-and-western songs, with three exceptions: "A Cub Fan's Dying Prayer," Sinatra's version of "Chicago," and "Angel of The Morning." She's always pumping quarters painted with red fingernail polish into the jukebox and pushing those three tunes. I can't count the number of times I've come into The Shortstop and heard her belting, "Just call me Angel of the morning, Angel. Just one more kiss before you leave me, baby." She thinks of The Short-stop as a family establishment, even though I'd fall off my stool if I ever saw a family walk through the door. Maybe a family of cockroaches or sewer-bred alligators. Definitely not a family of mammals.

When Angel returns with the Old Styles, Ivy pushes hers away and says, "I don't drink alcohol."

165

"Angel, this is Ivy," I say. "She comes from Cody, Illinois, the beefalo capital of the Midwest. It's ten miles south of Beloit."

"Blech!" says Ivy.

"What?"

"Beloit. I grew up with the name. It sounds like a quarter being dropped in a toilet. Beloit . . . Besides, I live in Chicago now."

"Yeah, she's a performance artist," I tell Angel.

"Pleased to meet you," she says.

"You want some pizza?" Ivy says.

"No, she doesn't want any pizza," I say, and put my hand on the lid.

"Domino's?" Angel says.

"It's not pizza," I say. "It's a squirrel."

"A squirrel."

"Yeah, a dead one."

"Pepperoni," Ivy says. "You want to see it, Angel?"

"Sure, why not?"

"No, you don't want to see it," I say. My hand is still on the lid.

Ivy looks sideways and gives me a half smile, a dare. Her look says "What's the big deal?" She's right. After all, Angel's not my mother.

With my job and all, I'm not easy to phase, but Ivy definitely phases me. Not only her actions, but the way she dresses. An orange scarf as big as window drapes. Black fishnet stockings and metallic silver lipstick. Usually my life is pretty dull, but around Ivy, I feel the way I do when I'm sitting on the pot and I hear the fans cheer in Wrigley Field.

"You ever had squirrel?" says Angel. "Tastes just like chicken. Of course, there ain't as much meat on a squirrel."

"Do you always believe what you see, Angel?" Ivy says.

"Almost never," says Angel, leaning towards her, a look of concentration on her face. "A fella come in here the other day selling keychains. He had a metal man and a metal woman on the keychain, and when he wiggled a lever they started doing things. He said he had a whole trunk-full in his car, and did I want to sell some on a card behind the counter? I said, 'Look around, this is a family place.' He said, 'You'd be surprised. People just love them. I've seen grandmas and young girls go crazy over them.' 'Yeah, well this is a gay bar, buddy,' I said. 'That's fine,' he said. 'I can take off the woman and put on another man. I already did that with one gay establishment. I'll put on dogs. I'll put on a man and a horse. Even two Japanese girls and a rhinoceros if that's what you want. Whatever turns you on.' Some people just want to shock you. I could have called the cops, but I ignored him. Eventually, he just slithered back under his rock."

"You want some pizza?" Ivy says.

"Yeah, why not?" says Angel.

I take my hand off the lid and wait for Ivy to open up the box, but she doesn't move. What's she waiting for? I wonder if I'm going nuts. If Ivy's brainwashing me. I've known her two days, and suddenly I want to show Angel the dead squirrel in the pizza box.

"One object can have many functions," Ivy says. "Consider this pizza box. For you and me, it signifies food. For Rocky the squirrel, it's his final resting place. When you put the two together, it's repulsive. Why? Because food and death are opposites, right? No, not at all. Food and death go hand in hand, but our escapist society allows us to blithely ignore that fact. Hold the mayo, hold the lettuce, special orders don't upset us. Right, Angel? Next time you go to an open casket funeral, don't be surprised if you see a pizza with the works lying there."

I have a strange feeling in my mouth. My tongue seems to be getting bigger. I've gone through my whole life barely noticing my tongue, and now, all of a sudden, it seems humongous. I can't figure out where to place it. I try to settle it down by my cheek. I stick it between my teeth.

Angel tucks her chin into her neck.

My tongue has swollen to the size of a blimp.

Still, I manage to say to Angel, "Ya wa thom peetha?"

"Sure, why not?" she says.

I open up the box and Angel shrinks back.

She gives me a look and I can already tell that she's cancelled me out as a regular. Now, I'm just another bar story: "You remember Rick? He came in here with a squirrel in a pizza box. Yeah, it was dead."

*I*vy shows up at work with me the next day. All she does is read poetry between stops, take notes, and draw sketches of the commuters. She's sort of nuts, but I like the way she looks at things. To her, everything's art. You can spit on the sidewalk and that's art. The commuters at rush hour are art, too. The way they crane their heads over the platform to see the train coming. They bob out as far as they can without sprawling onto the tracks. I've seen this sight everyday for ten years, but now Ivy tells me it's beautiful. Up and down the line, they wait, sticking their necks out. Ivy says they look like a bunch of pigeons jostling for breadcrumbs. All I see are some cranky people ready to be home.

When the doors open, they cram onto the car. At Washington, a couple more shove their way inside. At the next stop, Grand Ave., no one else can possibly fit, but a few try anyway, and the doors won't close. The button man and his friend are trying to jam on. He looks like he's added some buttons. Now they cover not only his chest, but his back, too. Over the intercom I say, "Clear the doors on car number five. Get in or get out and wait for the next train." Of course, no one except me has any idea which car's number five. But the button man and his friend are the ones who get off. As the doors close, I read some of his new buttons: "I Drink To Make Other People More Interesting," "No One Is Ugly After 2 A.M.," "It's Been Monday All Week," "Welcome To The Zoo," "The More People I Meet, The More I Like My Dog," "Beam Me Up Scotty . . . There Are No Virgins Left," "Only Visiting This Planet," "Art May Imitate Life, But Life Imitates Television," and "Time Flies When You Don't Know What You're Doing."

Ivy yells in my ear. "Now there's an artist! A walking circus."

"Yeah, a walking circus," I say, and laugh. "Las Vegas on a stick."

"That's perfect," she says, giving me a small hug. She puts what I just said into a notebook, writing in the tiniest print I've ever seen.

*A*ccording to Ivy, my apartment is art, too. Or, at least she'd like it to be. I'm not so sure, but I give her the run of the place anyway. I figure it can use some straightening, but Ivy goes a little overboard. She spends one whole weekend rummaging through the apartment, throwing out some things and rearranging others. Half of my memorabilia collection gets the boot. I hate getting rid of this stuff.

"What about these?" I say, showing her my three Buddha statues that I found on the El. She points to the largest of the Buddhas and says, "That's a keeper." She's sitting in the middle of the living room floor sorting through my memorabilia. In the throwaway pile is my African ebony hourglass, my Cubs briefcase, my AM/FM radio, and my Cubs cooler.

"I kind of think this is artistic, don't you?" I say, picking up my Cubs briefcase.

"It's up to you," she says. "I'm just making suggestions."

She looks so disappointed.

Later, I put the throwaway pile in a box and set it downstairs by the trash bin with a sign that reads, "Free."

I still haven't got the hang of all this.

*I*vy starts taking me to different installations. At one gallery a man toasts dozens of Pop Tarts while reading the Constitution. At another, a guy sits in the fetal position inside a three foot tall box. Outside is a video screen which shows him sitting there. After that, a woman in black pajamas lectures on nuclear war while pelting us with eggs. Then there's the Mystery Installation. No one knows where it is, who's the artist, or what's supposed to happen. Only the date. The flyer says simply "Coming April 17."

Installations

* * *

One night, we're sitting in the living room taking target practice at my Cuervo collection with my hand grenade lighter. I've given up drinking, and now we shatter a few bottles every night before turning in. I'm down to about a hundred.

The phone rings and I answer. "Is Ivy there?" a man's voice says hesitantly.

I point to Ivy and she points to herself. "Who is it?" Ivy says. In the five weeks that Ivy's been with me, no one's called her. She doesn't seem to have any friends. Only acquaintances. People in galleries who don't even seem to know her name, hug her and ask, "Where have you been hiding?" and move on before she has a chance to answer. Around most people Ivy acts stiff and angry, like she expects to be insulted. Only around me does she loosen up, though I'm not sure why. Sometimes I think we're pretty compatible, but sometimes I think she just needs a place to stay.

"Can I tell her who's calling?" I say to the man.

"Tell Ivy it's her parents," says the man. "We'd like to speak with her."

"Ivy, it's your parents."

"I have nothing to say to them," she says.

"Ivy, it's your parents," I repeat. "I can't tell them that."

Ivy shrugs. "Tell them I've turned into a dragonfly. When they learn to speak dragonfly I'll talk with them."

"We'd just like to speak with her, that's all," says her father. "Is she all right?"

"Yes, yes," I say. "She's fine." I put the receiver to

my chest and say, "Ivy, please. Speak with your folks. You can't not speak with your folks."

"Okay," she yells and leaps up from the couch. She rips the phone away from me and puts it to her ear. "Okay," she says to the phone.

After that she doesn't say anything for a minute.

"Okay, I won't hang up," she says finally.

She stands there holding the phone about six inches from her ear, like a snake dancer with a coiled rattler.

*A*s we're lying in bed that night, Ivy says, "I hope you're not too happy. I hope you're not enjoying yourself too much."

"Not in the least," I tell her. "I'm in agony. Don't touch me there. It's too agonizing."

Ivy takes her hand away.

"I was just kidding," I say. "I like a little agony from time to time."

One thing about this girl. She takes everything literally.

"The secret is staying off-balance," she says. "Whenever I start seeing someone, I immediately think of how we're going to break up. Then I'm happy. If I imagine the worst, then I can relax and enjoy myself."

"Here," I say, taking her hand. "Put your hand back there. I was just kidding."

"My parents think that it's wrong to cut yourself off from the people you've grown close to," she says, looking up at the ceiling and absentmindedly stroking me. "To me, it's just moving on, shedding skin."

"Yes, that's it," I say. "Yes. There. That feels good. No, I mean bad. It's right in between."

Installations

* * *

I start to give Ivy a hand with her installations. The first one's small, unplanned, but not quite spur-of-the-moment. We head for the Loop on a warm Sunday afternoon with a Lady Remington razor. I shave Ivy's head on the steps of the Art Institute. Then she shaves my head. This is one of the parts I hadn't planned. At first I'm thinking, "Wait a second," but then I see the surprised faces of the spectators: commuters every one of them. *I'm* doing something crazy now. Let someone else be the authority figure this time.

We gather our hair and arrange it around the head of one of the stone lions in front of the museum. Our goal is to transform the lion into Moe of the Stooges, but it's harder to get loose hair to stay in place than you might think. The bangs are the most difficult. Unfortunately, before we can get the head in shape, the wind scatters our clippings.

We've got a pretty good-sized crowd around us, maybe twenty people. A puppeteer, with not nearly as many onlookers, stands jealously on the steps by the other stone lion. We ignore him as he goes through his routine with his marionettes. He swivels them around, and the two puppets point and jeer at us. They're not the only ones. The crowd is on the ugly side. "There are better ways to get attention," one marionette yells. "Why do you do such disgusting things?" the other says. Most people just walk by without looking at us. Ivy says they're the ones who worry her the most, the people who don't notice.

* * *

*S*ometimes Ivy starts shivering when it's not even cold. When I touch her, she says, "You're always touching. I feel like bruised fruit." So I stop touching and she says, "You're so distant. You're the worst lover I've ever had. I've been having a lot of dreams about women lately." I try touching her again, but she's restless.

"What's going to make you happy?" I say. "Sacrificing a beefalo? A vat of putrefying squirrels?"

She's alert again and smiling. I meant the question as an insult, but she looks like she expected it.

"Commuting at the speed of art," she says like this is the only possible answer.

*I*t's hard to tell the audience from the passengers tonight. They're all audience, I guess. I'm off-duty, but I'm wearing my conductor's uniform. I go up to the real conductor, a guy named Fred, and explain what we're doing. He just twists his mouth and stares at me. I ask him what his problem is and he says, "What happened to your hair? Didn't you used to have hair?"

"I shaved it for an installation," I tell him.

He twists his mouth again.

"Never mind," I say. "Here's twenty bucks. Just leave us alone for half an hour, okay?"

"Okay," he says. "But I still got to know what it is. I could lose my job. So could you."

"It's just art," I tell him. "Nothing to worry about."

"Well, okay then," and he walks off with the twenty I've handed him.

The train's moving steady at about 30 mph. I keep my hand on the back of one of the seats as we rock back and forth. We round a corner and sparks shoot up from our wheels.

I get on the intercom and announce, "Hello, you miserable commuters. This is Jason, your conductor from hell. No smoking, littering, or radio playing allowed."

About twenty of the passengers smile at me. The other ten keep their eyes in front of them as though they're soldiers in foxholes waiting for an assault. Good, I've got their attention. Now I can tell who the audience is and who the real commuters are. One young child balances in the middle of the aisle. "Carlos, *ven aca!*" his mother yells from three seats back. She's got four other children gathered in two seats around her. She's about seven months pregnant and wears a blue T-shirt with dark smears on it. The T-shirt has a picture of a bulldog and reads, "YALE."

Carlos doesn't hear his mother or doesn't want to obey. He bends down and picks up something invisible from the floor. Then he rubs it while squatting and rocking to the rhythm of the train.

"Carlos!" the woman yells again and darts out into the aisle and snatches the kid. She dangles him by an arm and swats him loudly.

Then she gives me a look like I was the one who made Carlos disobey. Like I want Carlos to be a juvenile delinquent. Like I was the one who just smacked him.

A little late, Ivy enters the car from the door at the other end. She looks as pregnant as the woman with the Yale T-shirt. She's carrying two shopping bags and she wears a platinum blond wig with a huge patch torn out of the scalp. Ivy closes the door behind her and starts waddling down the center aisle. Most of the passengers turn around and watch.

When she's halfway up the aisle, she squirms in her dress and moans. She reaches into one of her bags, takes out a turkey baster, and squirts it at the person sitting in the seat nearest her. A stream of milk trickles onto the man's crotch. The man looks at her and barks twice. Most likely he's one of the people she invited to the installation, but it's hard to tell. I've seen regular passengers bark before.

"Excuse me, miss," I yell down the aisle. "No smoking, littering, or radio playing allowed. No turkey basting."

The woman in the Yale T-shirt cranes her neck into the aisle and looks at Ivy. Then she puts her arms around her two closest children.

Ivy sticks her turkey baster back into her shopping bag and keeps walking up the aisle.

After she's gone about five feet, she moans again and starts rubbing her pregnant-looking belly. "Oh my," she yells. "I feel it! I think I feel it!"

She takes another step and something slips between her legs and plops with a wet slap onto the floor.

Ivy steps back and reveals a slab of uncooked liver lying at her feet. Quickly, she snatches it up. "Get back here, you little rascal. You ain't incubated long enough yet." She stuffs the slab of liver back into her dress.

"Miss," I yell, "No smoking, littering, radio playing, turkey basting, or liver deliveries allowed."

The train approaches the station. As it slows down, the woman in the Yale T-shirt gathers her children around her. She pushes the five of them in front of her, her arms sweeping them along, her eyes fixed on Ivy.

Installations

Ivy stands in her way. The woman, frantically try-ing to get around her as the train stops, knocks into Ivy, who loses her balance momentarily and staggers back-wards as the train lurches to a standstill.

With a sucking sound, the rest of Ivy's fake preg-nancy slithers out her dress. The whole mess slops on the floor. Chicken gizzards and bloody cow and pig entrails. Ivy looks as surprised as anyone because this was supposed to happen gradually.

The doors open, but the woman stands there a moment looking straight at Ivy and spits, *"Puta!"*

Then she herds her children out the doors. About five other people push through the doors with her. Undaunted, Ivy chases them off the train by squirting them in the back with her turkey baster.

Fred, in the next car, closes the doors and we start up again.

I hear someone pounding on the doors. The woman in the T-shirt raps with her knuckles, her face twisted, her mouth open, her eyes pleading.

"What is it?" I say.

We gather speed, and she falls away from the door like someone being hooked off a stage. As she crum-ples, I hear the scream. "Carlos!" she yells.

I turn around and see Carlos kneeling, playing with the fallen gizzards. He looks up and displays his hands to me as though I'm his father and he's just washed up for dinner. He's covered with chicken and beef blood. The boy puts his fingers in his mouth and giggles.

*I*vy thinks it's funny and stupid that someone would forget her own kid on the train. Ivy's friends think it's part of the installation. I take a minute to react, but then I pull the emergency cord. The brakes echo the mother's scream. I run to get Fred and tell him to head back. He starts yelling and says he's going to report me, that I'm definitely going to lose my job.

After we reunite Carlos with his mother, Ivy and her friends traipse off to Angel's Shortstop for after-installation drinks. "You'll love this place," Ivy tells her friends. Poor Angel.

I'm left alone on the platform with the woman and her kids. The woman yells while her kids look up at me in awe. I listen even though I can't understand a word she's saying. I just stand there while she yells. She keeps this up for longer than is possible for one person to yell at another. The train leaves. Ten minutes later another train pulls into the station. She keeps yelling. But I stand here and take it. Finally, she herds her kids away and leaves me.

I stand alone on the platform at Addison for a while, facing Wrigley Field. I start pacing back and forth. I walk to the edge of the platform, where it narrows into a point and signs warn of the danger of electrocuting yourself. My life is ruined. In an alley below me a black dog trots between the garbage cans. Past the alley and before Wrigley Field, there's a large parking lot. A couple of apartment buildings stand on either side. A poster on one of the buildings shows Harry Caray with his butterball head, thick glasses, and uncontained joy, leaping through space. His arm is raised as though he's about to lead the crowd at Wrigley Field during the seventh inning stretch: "Okay now, let's hear it! Take me out to the ballgame!"

Installations

Bold letters below him pronounce: "CUB FAN, BUD MAN"

A boy about ten, who's drunk or pretending to be, staggers down Sheffield, grabbing a lamp post and twirling around. He does a strange limbery Watusi down the sidewalk. No one else is around and he doesn't know I'm watching. Who does he think he's doing this dance for?

"Hey! You!" I yell, but he doesn't hear, or pretends not to.

In a minute he's turned the corner and is gone.

A cannon burst, a sonic boom. Then the sound of thousands of wind chimes buffeted in a typhoon.

Glass is flying all over the parking lot from the building with the Harry Caray poster. It takes me a second to realize what's going on, but then I see the windows of the building have been blown out. A gas explosion, a bomb factory, a huge shotgun blast. Who knows?

A group of teenagers dashes out of the building and into the lot.

Someone runs from the building on the other side of the lot and yells, "Hey, is everything cool? Is everything cool?"

A man clambers out of a window by Harry Caray's knee. He swims, two quick overhead strokes before he hits the ground. Two kids climb over the fence at the back of the building. All over the parking lot, people are running around yelling, "What happened? Is everything cool?"

I hear a laugh, or maybe it's a cry. It comes from the building, and someone's yelling, "Did you call them? Are they coming?"

I feel so clear-headed as they run around. I look out towards the lakefront with its apartment complexes all

179

lit up, and what am I thinking about? Water. A drop of it falling on the third rail. Worlds within worlds sizzling within that drop. A black dog trotting between cans, living off garbage. A drunken boy doing a strange Watusi. Harry Caray leaping joyfully through the abyss. This clear agony I'm feeling. I'm thinking about Ivy touching me, the rash she's given me, the skin I've shed. I feel like a tunnel with wind rushing through it. I feel like an underground test, a needle pointing to a zone past measurement.

I turn around again and lean over the railing of the El. Below me stands a cluster of kids, watching an orange flame bend a window.

"Hey. Hey you!" I yell.

All of them turn around at once and stare. They're looking up at me so expectantly, their eyes wide, their faces ready to receive.

"Did you see that?" I yell down to them. "Did you SEE that?"

ROBIN HEMLEY was born in New York City in 1958. His work has appeared in many small magazines and in *20 Under 30: Best Short Stories by America's New Young Writers*. He lives in Charlotte, North Carolina, where he is at work on a novel.